SAVING APRIL

SARAH A. DENZIL

SAVING APRIL

Sarah A. Denzil

Cover Design by Damons

PROLOGUE

She ran down the drive in her bare feet and dressing gown. Her hair was whipped up by the wind, the strands flowing out behind her. Her small soles slapped the tarmac. She felt the slice of her flesh on the stones, but she didn't care. She had to keep going. There was a wild expression in her eyes, the kind that's only seen in the utterly terrified. Her dressing gown came loose as she ran, spreading out like wings. She focussed on getting away from the house. She focussed on the man. He was dead ahead, and she was going to run into his arms. He was wearing reflective gear, and he had his arms outstretched, waiting for her. She allowed herself one brief moment to glance behind her for a final time. When she turned back towards the man, she felt the heat on her skin, still tingling, still smouldering. Her small body folded into his arms, and she was safe.

HANNAH

Cavendish Street is like any other residential road in the suburbs. It appears a little worn at first glance, but when you really scrutinise the place, you start to notice how much strength there is beneath the surface. The terraced houses are old and Victorian. The pavement is unyielding. There are tough faces staring out from behind the panes of glass. A few roads down looms a cold copse of trees on the outskirts of a wood. The streets are bare on the way into the small shopping area. There's a dirty, run down park with a single swing in it.

In the summer months, the smell of roast dinners floats down from number 68. The residents of Cavendish Street open their windows, letting their flavours out into the muggy air. My mouth waters as I poke at the plate of oily noodles resting on my knees. But worse still, the smell of beef gravy brings back memories I'd rather forget, of a different time and place, where I had an oak table and a white table cloth and laughed until my abdomen cramped. Then comes the sound of Edith Clarke's phlegmy cough and I'm back at number 73 with chicken stir fry on my lap, and a radio play about farmers blaring out in the background.

The road is narrow, so that the houses almost lean over the pavement. Tall and sturdy, they stand like judgemental parents, with their large windows offering a peek into the lives beyond brick, shaming you into glancing swiftly away, rather than lingering on the pot plants and ornaments, or whatever TV programme is on; glimpses into the lives of others. The front door is in the living room, and it opens straight onto the pavement. I often sit on the sofa and watch the joggers go past, meeting each eye, daring them to stare. The back door opens into the kitchen. Beyond that, you're forced to share a garden with your neighbour. Good old Edith, with her milky eyes and smoker's cough. She keeps the whole thing tip-top while I sip wine on the door step. She potters and fusses around, adding garden gnomes to her ever growing collection, telling me about the gossip from the other houses—72 has been sold, and the paperwork is in motion, the couple at 65 are divorcing, there are rumours he had an affair—while her old bones shuffle along, veiny hands clutching the watering can.

Edith's husband died before I moved to Cavendish Street. She's lived here all her life and likes to tell me about it. *When George was alive... Before all those foreigners moved in... I never used to lock my door, y'know. I knew everyone on the street by name. Everyone.* I smile and nod and tell myself that it's good to listen to another human being. I spend so much time on my own that there are days where I don't even speak aloud. So in these fleeting summer months, I force myself to sit outside and listen to whatever Edith has to say, whether it's generational racism or a boring story about her trip to the doctor's. But today I can't even face Edith. My hands have been shaking all afternoon, and the noodles slither off the trembling fork before reaching my mouth. My thoughts are black. Everything is something to be afraid of: the slight niggle in my calf is a blood clot, the heartburn is a heart attack, the headache is a brain tumour. I have to place down my fork and take a deep breath. In and out, in and out.

"Hannah, you are not dying," I say. There, I spoke today. It was to myself, but I spoke. "There is nothing wrong with you. Eat your noodles."

Cavendish Street is more than the place I live, it's my whole world. There was a time when the entire planet was my whole world, but I stopped going abroad years ago. Gradually, my world shrank smaller and smaller until the end of the street felt like a marathon. And it's not something I consciously changed. It just sort of happened, like a habit I rerouted. It's so easy to stay in now. I can order anything online. I work from home. I have a treadmill and a bike in the spare bedroom that serves as my office (they gather dust, but I have them for the times I begin to panic about having a stroke in my forties). There's only me so the bills are inexpensive, and I can make a living writing articles and editing stories for clients. It's not so bad, really. I have a trip to the co-op on the days where I feel up to it, when the world doesn't seem to be imploding on top of me and pushing me down until I can't breathe.

I sigh and stand up. The noodles will have to go. I'm too wired to eat. I scrape the cold, congealed mess into the bin and rinse the plate under the tap. The water spurts out twice before flowing, which I should get fixed but never feel like arranging. I don't like people in my house. I hate the gas men who appear unannounced, waving their lanyards in my face and calling me love. I hate the sound of knuckles on the door, and the people who ignore the doorbell or my polite request for visitors to use the back door. The letterbox jars me on the days I'm not expecting mail-order books or catalogue bras. The loud *thunk* has my heart pattering beneath my cardigan.

There's too much noise in this place. The radio is off with a click from my jerking finger, then the window is slammed shut, trapping me in a house that smells like soy sauce and oil. At least it blocks the sound of the baby crying three doors up.

I need a distraction from this creeping anxiety. I know the warning signs now. I know to watch out for the waves of panic and the dark thoughts, but what I don't know is how to stop it for good. So I turn back to the kitchen, pour a finger of chilled vodka into a tumbler, and turn on the kitchen taps to finish the washing up. The vodka is gone before the sink is full of water.

Pan scraped, plate cleaned, cutlery placed on the drainer. I'm not a natural cleaner, but the chore is familiar and reassuring. My shoulders drop a little as I'm drying my hands on the tea towel. But then there's some commotion outside that catches my attention.

For the last month, all Edith has talked about is the potential new owners of Number 72, the house directly opposite mine. Edith is obsessed with this house, because the last owner died. Every time I think about it, I shiver. There was nothing unusual. Not in the way he died. The old guy was in his seventies and had a heart attack sat in his armchair. His name was Derek. He'd always seemed like a kind man, even though we didn't really talk. Every now and then he would wave to me through the window, and he used to chat to Edith on his way to the co-op.

What's unsettling is how he was found. His son's family —including two children under ten—walked in to find a three-day-old corpse sat upright on the antique velvet armchair.

I shudder. If Derek had died anywhere else I probably would have seen his body and called an ambulance. But his grey head poking up above the back of the armchair was a normal sight for me. He could have been taking a nap, or watching television. I don't spend a whole lot of time in my living room—I'm usually in my office on the other side of the house—otherwise I might have noticed that he hadn't moved. The whole thing shook me up. I still feel guilty. I often peek into that house—which is empty and redecorated—and wonder if I hadn't been so caught up in my own problems that I might have spared the family that last trauma.

But then, sometimes our problems aren't so easy to set aside. Sometimes they cling on to us, filling us up until we can't see anything else.

I shake the thoughts out of my head and move into the living room. Edith will be pleased, because finally she can stop speculating about who will be moving into 72, and actually see for herself. The thought of her net curtain twitching makes me smile. I imagine her pretending to polish the window sill ornaments so she can get a good view.

But who am I to judge, because I stand here gawking myself.

The removal men are in blue overalls and they hop up

and down from the lorry in large work boots. Box after box is taken in through the doorway, and I can't help thinking of those boots trampling all over Derek's house, over the spot where he died. Another wave of guilt-fuelled panic washes over me, but I force it back down. A woman hops out of the house, weaving around the removal men, and opens a four-by-four parked behind the lorry. Hah! Edith won't be happy about that. She's always complaining about her daughter not being able to find a parking spot. Another large vehicle on the street will make the situation even worse. Then I remember my own car parked outside my house, the one that hasn't moved for over a year, and I realise that more hints about me selling it will fly my way.

The woman is petite, moves on her tip toes, and smiles at everyone in her path. I get that jolt of female jealousy. That pointless competitiveness that makes us compare ourselves to others. She's far prettier, far slimmer, and seems altogether nicer than I am. But even still, there is nothing too remarkable about her. She doesn't dye her hair; it's a mousy brown rather than a highlighted blonde. She's wearing jeans and an over-sized shirt, though what I expect someone to wear when moving house, I don't know. It's not exactly going to be a ball gown. Her head disappears into the car, while she rummages around on the back seat. As she's half in the car, with her backside sticking out, at least two of the removal men hazard a glance in its direction. I actually make a strange noise of disgust, like I can't believe that those men are ogling her. But then I realise they aren't really ogling her. They didn't say or do anything. They just checked her out for a second. It's me. I'm jealous. When was the last time a man looked at me like that? I don't remember.

The man I presume to be her husband, or boyfriend, strides out of the house. He's in jeans and a T-shirt, which is stretched across a muscular chest. It's not the kind of body I find attractive on a man, it's too wide, too bulgy, like the kind built from extensive weight training. His skin has a red tinge to it, and his hair is cut into one of those fashionable "wedge" styles that footballers have caught onto. A strange hooligan form of smart 50s cut. He grabs the woman around the waist and drags her back. I take a step back, surprised by the almost aggressive action. She kicks out her legs, squirming in his arms, and my heartbeat quickens with a sort of voyeur anxiety. But then he puts her down and she spins around and slaps him hard on the arm. The guy laughs—I can hear the laughter through the window—before flicking her on the shoulder. I let out a long breath, realising that the two of them are being playful. For a moment I smile along with them.

But it's not my joke to laugh at. I move away from the window, suddenly aware of how intrusive I'm being.

I'm about to leave the new owners to unpack without my rubbernecking, when a young girl steps out from the house. The sight of her makes my stomach lurch. She's around twelve, maybe thirteen years old, and she walks with a stiff back. Her hair is long, and dark—almost black—and flows over her shoulders and rests down her back. She stops walking, stands on the pavement with her back to me, and then turns slowly towards my house. The panic rises up once again. I clench my fists and let out a little gasp. I want to move away from the window but my feet stay planted to the floor. The girl is pretty, but she has a serious face. For a brief moment, I feel protective when I think about all the people who will tell her to smile more, who will pinch her cheek and say "you're pretty when you smile". I shake my head and force those thoughts away. She's not my child to be protective about.

Slowly, the girl raises one hand and waves at me. I back away from the window and shut the curtains.

LAURA

I thought the grin was going to freeze on my face. Shutting the door and saying goodbye to the removal men is at least some relief, but now I'm stuck with a house that's a mess, and all our stuff packed in layers of bubble wrap. My arms ache, my legs ache, I'm filthy and sweaty.

"I'll call a pizza, babe," Matt says.

It's all right for him, he loves all this. He loves the excitement of moving somewhere new. The man can never settle in one place. This is our third home now, the second since April came along. Every five years we end up moving, because Matt gets those itchy feet again. I keep telling myself that if we move house, he won't use those itchy feet to run off, and at least then I'll be keeping my family together.

"We don't know any of the local places," I point out. I move around as I speak, banging cutlery into drawers, stuffing packaging into bin bags.

"There's always a Pizza Hut nearby. We're not that far out of the city," he replies, trying to cover the note of irritation in his voice, but failing as always. I'm the negative one who drags the atmosphere down. At least that's what I'm told.

"Where's April? She should be helping us." My voice sounds squeaky. I'm trying so hard not to let my thoughts darken my spirit, or at least not to let Matt see it.

"I said she could unpack her clothes." Matt sees my shoulders sag, and puts his mobile down on top of a box marked "living room stuff". "Hey, come here. Come on." He opens his arms out wide and gestures with his fingers. I let myself fold into his arms, but not before I put down the tea towel I was holding. "I know you're stressed, but it's for a good reason, the best reason. It's a new start for us."

A new start. A new start. That's just repackaged speak for change. A change where we move into a smaller house and Matt quits his job. I sigh, and try not to think about it, pressing my face into his chest. It never used to be so bumpy. A little over a year ago Matt thought he was too fat—even though he wasn't, he had a little late-30s spread developing, that's all—and started going to the gym. It became some sort of obsession, until he decided that he wanted to quit his office job and set up as a personal trainer. I encouraged him, of course. He's my husband; I want him to be happy. But it put a lot of strain on me and my job. I'm the provider now, the person who pays all the bills. Matt's job never brought in a lot, but it allowed us a comfortable buffer. It meant we got a holiday every year and new clothes when we felt like it. The problem was, we carried on with the new clothes and the holiday after Matt quit, and every month he had a new lead or a potential client, but somehow it never worked out.

"We're going to be happy here," he says. "We're a family."

When I move my head away, I hear the sound of quiet feet

on the stairs. April is coming down. She moves too slowly for a thirteen-year-old girl. She should be hopping around, dancing and bright like the girls in her class. But she's nothing like them, and that's something else I have to worry about.

"April, come and help me in the kitchen. There's lots to pack away."

Her dark hair appears around the door first. Then there are shoulders and a head. She blinks at me, not responding, still half hiding behind the door. She always reminds me of a fairy or a fawn in a Disney film, nervous and jumpy, likely to take flight if you get too close.

"April?" I say, in a voice that has a slight warning to it. "You need to help us unpack. You can't just stay in your room all day."

"Why not?" she asks, twirling a naked foot over the kitchen floor. Brand new flooring, as Matt has reminded me three times today. The recent renovation was one of the many aspects of this house that attracted us—mainly Matt—to the property.

Matt ruffles her hair and leans in close to her ear. "Because the monster in the wardrobe will get ya!"

I half sigh, half smile. He treats her too much like a little girl sometimes, but I must admit that it's nice to see April smile. She slinks around Matt and towards me, the smile being replaced by a more pensive expression. I worry about her odd, thoughtful expressions, but then I worry a lot about April. Like I worry about the way she has more of a relationship with Matt. I'm at work all day, often coming home late in the evening. Matt is at home all day, and now with the summer holidays in full swing, he gets to spend all day with April. How can I compete with that?

"What do you think of the new house then?" I ask, softening my voice. I pass her an unwrapped plate and gesture to the appropriate cupboard. "Pretty swanky, eh?"

"I guess," she replies with a half-hearted shrug.

"You'll love it once we're settled," Matt says, grinning. He leans on the breakfast bar—brand new—and taps the surface with his fingers.

"How come Dad's lazing around over there and not helping?" I say, trying to make a joke but hearing it fall flat to even my ears. "Come on, get your arse over here and put those pots away."

Matt salutes me with gusto, and says, "Aye, aye, captain. Christ, your mum's a right stickler." The "right" inflecting with his Northern twang to sound more like "rate".

I watch the two of them start unpacking another box and know that I should be happy. Not everyone has a beautiful family, a good career, and a few half decent friends. Some people live alone with none of those things, not even a healthy body. But that happiness is as nervous as April herself, and, like the fairies in a Disney film, it can't be coaxed to the surface if it doesn't want to emerge. I stand there smiling, but all I can think about it is how *it doesn't seem real*. And that unsettles me to the very marrow of my bones.

"What about that pizza then?" Matt says. He's busier poking April in the side than he is helping with the unpacking.

"Hmm?" I mumble.

Before Matt can speak, the doorbell goes. I frown at Matt before putting down an unpacked bowl and moving into the living room. I'm not particularly happy about how there's not even a hallway between the living room and the front door. I hate how it opens onto the street, it feels too intimate some-how. But once again, I swallow my concerns. Matt said I'd get used to it, so maybe I will.

"Oh, hello."

An elderly woman stands on the doorstep. The incline of the street, and the way the houses are a little raised and set back, makes me feel like a giant compared to her tiny frame.

"Hello," I reply.

She lifts a casserole dish with a tea towel covering it, and smiles through lipstick stained teeth. I take the dish from her, trying to arrange my face into an expression that resembles gratitude.

"I'm Edith, I live at 75. I wanted to welcome you to the street," she says.

I lift the tea towel and examine the contents. There are a few unappetising buns piled up inside the dish. I try not to grimace at the dry texture and flat appearance.

"That's so kind, thank you. I'm Laura, my husband is Matt, and we have a thirteen-year-old daughter called April. I'm sure we're going to be very happy here. It seems really friendly."

"Oh it is," she says, almost with some force. Her face is made up, despite the deep crevices, which gives her a slightly ridiculous and almost creepy appearance. I can't stop staring at the mascara clumping in the corner of her eye, or the way her lipstick trails off at one side. "At one time I knew the name of everyone on this street. It's still friendly, but the community isn't quite the same. We used to look after each other, you see. That's how it was in them days. It's a shame really. If things had stayed the same, I doubt Derek would have died like that." She wrings her veiny hands together and purses her lips.

"Oh, I'm sorry, I didn't realise there had been a death. Was he a friend of yours?" I ask, wondering how quickly I can get the conversation to end without appearing rude.

"Lovely man, he was. Salt of the Earth. Would have done anything for you. It weren't right, you know. A man like that shouldn't pass away and no one notice for three days. I was with my daughter at the time so I couldn't know, but her across the street didn't even notice. Too busy in her own life, I reckon. She's the selfish sort."

My eyes flick towards the house directly opposite. I could swear that I see a quick flash of movement, but whatever it is disappears as quickly as it appeared.

"You mean... he died in this house?" I say, suddenly horrified.

"In his armchair, he was," she continues, either ignoring or not noticing my discomfort. "Right in front of the window. How she didn't even see him I don't know. Ended up that his family found him three days later when they came to bring him his shopping. Awful it was."

"How terrible," I say, feeling my muscles tense. It really was terrible. The whole story made my skin crawl. I feel a sudden dislike for this woman coming to my house on our moving in day and telling us such a horrific story. I want her to leave, to get away from us.

"Well I'd best be getting on," she says. She coughs into her fist, and I hear the sound of phlegm on her chest. "This sunny weather is wonderful, but it means even more watering the garden." She tuts and rolls her eyes. "Of course her next door never does any gardening. She just sits there with a bottle of wine and watches old muggins here get on with it. Welcome to the neighbourhood." She leans forward and grasps my arm with her claw-like hand. "We watch out for each other here now. We learnt a lesson when Derek died. No one should be going through all that and not get help."

My mouth opens and closes like a vacant fish as I struggle to find an appropriate response. But before I can, Edith has scuttled down the front steps and is across the road, moving pretty swiftly for an old woman. I imagine she's made of the toughest stuff, forged by wartime spirit and childbirth and mining husbands and everything else those Northern women are made from.

"Bye," I say, before backing away and locking the door.

"What was all that about?" Matt asks.

I hold out the dish. "One of the neighbours brought us these."

Matt gives me an I-told-you-so smile. "See, nothing bad happens in this street. This is our perfect new start."

I smile. If I keep smiling, maybe I'll believe him.

HANNAH

I'm not sure how it happened, whether it was gradual or sudden, but now I blend into the house like a piece of background furniture. Pets and owners start to resemble each other if they develop an over-attached relationship. Well I'm like that with my house. The walls were once a light shade of cream but they appear to have faded into an almost grey colour that matches my skin. I chose brown curtains when I first moved in, and it's only now that I see the mud colour of my hair and eyes. Even the furnishings—which I chose in different shades of purple and mauve—are the same colour as most of my clothes. There's a haphazard, untidy feel to the place, the same sight I see when I examine my messy waves of curls in the mirror.

We're both a little bloated, a little cluttered, and out of fashion. We're both unkempt and slightly dirty. Neither of us live up to our potential. We're a little uncared for. A little sad. That's how an estate agent would describe my house to potential buyers "It's a bit sad right now, but with some updating it could be very homely." And that's how a pimp would describe me. "I'm not gonna lie, she's getting on a bit now, you know those late-thirties types, but show her a good time and she'll come round."

The thing about working from home alone, is that you think about these things. You think about all sorts, from uplifting visions of the future where you get your shit together and everything works out, to the absolute worst scenario where everything goes wrong, to imagining your own death—the mundanity of choking on a peanut or falling down the stairs, to the absurd home invasion by a serial killer —but most of all you dredge up old memories that you try so hard to keep locked away. And it's this that keeps me up at night and wakes me up before the sun begins to rise.

That's why I end up checking my Fiverr account at five in the morning. Edith's coughs told me she was up by six, so I decided to make myself a strawberry and banana smoothie and switch the fan on. I check the thermostat on the wall and the temperature is already 21 degrees. I open the window, and sit down on the sofa with my laptop on my knees, checking to see if I have any more clients on Fiverr. My account states that I'll edit and proofread short stories for £30, and I can get quite a few done in a day. I have one story to finish but I'm putting it off. The thought of finishing it makes me tense.

I have one rule when it comes to choosing the stories I proofread—they can't contain violence or horror. I can't stand reading stories with blood and guts in them. It triggers a stirring within me, an emotion that I would much rather keep buried. But I let one slip by, a story about a predator stalking a little girl, and every time I try to read it, I feel the same dark panic seeping through my veins. Then the flashes of disturbing memories come; snapshots into a past I'd rather forget.

My body is coiled up tight this morning, so I put the laptop aside and stretch my legs by walking around the room. There's movement across the road. The Masons are up. I know all their names now, thanks to Edith. It didn't take her long to go snooping over there. The husband is Matt Mason, but she doesn't know what he does, not yet. The wife—the pretty woman with mousey hair—is Laura, and their thirteen-year-old daughter is April. Pretty name that, April. The kind of name that sounds good for a young girl and an older woman. So many parents choose cutesy names for their children without thinking of what it would be like for them as an adult. I guess these are the people who start using their middle name, or shorten their first name to a more appropriate nickname. I'd always been a bit jealous of the kids at school who went by their middle name. They were more grown up to me. But, no, I had the most mundane of names—Hannah. A palindrome. A safe bet. You can't tease a silly nickname out of Hannah Abbott. It's too boring.

As I'm reaching the dregs of my smoothie, and am considering picking up the stalker story again, I hear a noise that sounds a lot like shouting. With it being so warm this morning, I'd opened the living room window, and now someone's argument is seeping in along with the still air. The voices are deep and angry. I know I shouldn't, but I can't help it, I move closer to the window, drawing back the curtains and letting the low sun light up the dreary room. The voices are coming from the house across the street. Inside, the Masons are yelling at each other with complete abandon. I can just make out the shape of their bodies. Laura stands in the centre of the room while Matt paces around her, his large, bulky man-shape prowling like some sort of beast. I'm immediately intimidated by him, by the fury in his voice, and the way he eats up the room with his presence.

Laura speaks, and I can hear the tears in her voice. There's a high-pitched hint of hysteria (a term I hate, but that best describes the desperation and anger mixed in her voice). I take another step towards the window, listening as closely as I can. I make out "you're not listening, we can't, we can't." Soon after, Matt storms out of the house with a duffel bag over his shoulder. I step back, ducking around the curtain so he won't see me. He runs a hand through his hair, shrugs his shoulders, and stalks off up the road, not even bothering to get in the car.

It's Laura who slams the door behind him. She disappears from the living room, probably into the kitchen. I'm about to move away from the window and shut the curtains so I can pretend that I didn't intentionally try to overhear someone else's argument, but there is movement from the top floor of the house. I look up to see April Mason standing in the window. I pity her in that moment. She's awake and could have heard the whole argument, seeing as most likely the entire street heard it. She stands there in patterned pyjamas and long black hair, and she waves to me. After a brief hesitation, I wave back.

When I move away from the window, I can't help but feel shocked. The Masons are so different to what I'd imagined. I think of Matt Mason putting his thick arms around Laura's middle and Laura play-hitting his shoulder. How can the same couple be screaming and slamming doors the next day? It makes me wonder whether we can really know a person, and really understand what goes on behind closed doors.

They had another fight this morning. I thought about hiding, but then I heard the door slam, so I knew Dad left. I think the fight was about me, because I kept hearing my name. It started off with them loud whispering, trying not to wake me up. Then Dad was shouting and Mum was crying, and I started to get afraid again. I hate it when they fight, but I hate it more when Dad gets angry. I hate it so very much that it makes me cry. I cry and I try not to think about it, try not to think what he does to me and Mum.

LAURA

My fingers shake as I switch on the kettle for a cup of tea. I glance at my watch, it's almost 7:30, I wonder if I should make a start on April's breakfast. When we've been fighting like this, I feel so guilty that I make her something special. What will it be today? Ready Brek or a bacon sandwich. She used to love Ready Brek when she was little, sprinkled with some sugar or a dollop of honey. But now, I'm not so sure. Now that she's on the cusp of becoming a teenager, I can't second guess what she wants or needs anymore.

Am I a bad mother? Matt certainly thinks I am. You would think I am judging from the way he screams at me about her schooling. The problem with Matt is that he wants the best for everything but he has no solution on how to get it. Then all of his anger and frustrations come out on me. I hold back a sob, thinking of the way he was screaming at me. I was frightened. I'll admit it, I was actually frightened. I felt myself almost shutting down, closing in on myself while he stalked around the room, puffed up and red like a madman.

He wants April to go to a private school, but there is no way in hell we can afford it. My income has to support everything right now: the mortgage, the bills, our food, everything. We've downsized because of it. But even now Matt thinks he's going to get clients, and that he's going to earn a fortune from personal training. But these clients never actually materialise. It's always "I'm so close, babe. I know he's going to sign. You should see his car, he's loaded!" but then nothing happens and Matt goes into another depression. During these bouts of moodiness, he spends all his free time in the gym, punishing me by leaving as soon as I walk through the door. "You missed tea," he'll say, as I walk in from work. "It's in the microwave, you can heat it up." Most nights I eat my microwaved food in front of the telly with April upstairs in her room reading or doing homework.

Who knew that having a family could make you so lonely? It's supposed to fix that, isn't it? That's why we had a child, to make sure we'd never be lonely again. But now I know the real truth—that having a family doesn't solve everything. A child won't automatically become your friend. I'm in this cycle where I work so hard to keep my family that I never see them. While I'm working this hard I'm actually pushing them all away.

I have to brush away tears before pouring the milk over the soft flakes of Ready Brek. I don't care if she's too old for it, that's what I'm making, and maybe if I make it, I can force her to be a child for a little while longer.

"April?" I call. "I'm making you breakfast, do you want to come down?"

Maybe I should put some bacon on just in case? I shake my head. No point wasting food. She probably won't want it.

Kids are different now to when I was a teen, they're more health conscious. April makes me trim the fat off the bacon, and insists on brown bread with only a tiny bit of butter. "I don't want my arteries clogged up," she says.

I shove the bowl with the Ready Brek into the brand new microwave that Matt insisted we buy, like the brand new kettle and toaster, and the new coffee table. We had a frantic day unpacking and building furniture yesterday. I should have known a blazing row was coming from the way we bickered and picked at each other. I wasn't holding the leg of the coffee table right so he couldn't screw in the last screw. And I dropped a vase, the most expensive one. That's usually what it's like with Matt, all these little things build up until he explodes.

I turn around and almost scream. "April! Jesus, you gave me a fright."

She moves a box from off the breakfast bar and sits down, still in her pyjamas. The girl has silent footsteps and an unnerving way of slinking through the house.

"I'm making you Ready Brek. Would you like some sugar on top?"

She shakes her head. "Have we got any strawberries?"

I open the fridge door and have a rummage around. "No strawberries, but we have blueberries, will those do?" I stocked up on a few things after getting the pizza last night. The takeaway made me feel so bloated and sluggish that I decided we needed real food in the house. Plus, I couldn't sleep, so went for a drive across our old neighbourhood to the late night Tesco in town.

The microwave dings. I gingerly remove the hot bowl, stir, and sprinkle blueberries on top. Then I push the bowl of steaming hot food towards April before working on my cup of tea.

"Did you sleep okay? How's the new room?"

"It's all right," she says. "I like watching the street."

"Doing a little people watching?" I smile. It's rare for April to tell me her likes and dislikes. I usually get a grunt or a shrug.

"And listening," she says. "You can hear people on the street talking and stuff. That old lady likes to talk a lot."

The smile fades from my face. What must the new neighbours think of us? We've only been in the house a day, and already we've had a blazing row.

"She's nosy," April continues. "She keeps talking about us. I can't hear what she's saying because she lowers her voice, but I see her watching our house."

Great, that's exactly what we don't need, a gossipy old woman up in our business. "Ignore her, honey. Some people don't have much of a life of their own so they spy on others'. So, are you excited about starting a new school in September?"

At this question, I see her physically tense. A flush of heat spreads up to my face, she heard us arguing.

She pokes at a blueberry and stares down at the bowl in front of her. "I don't mind where I go to school."

"I know, sweetheart." There's a catch in my throat. I never meant for her to get mixed up in mine and Matt's problems. I should learn by now how to hide it better, how to stop Matt from... from his rages.

HANNAH

Sometimes I make deals with myself. I bribe myself. If I can get through the next ten minutes, the following ten minutes won't be half as hard. Sometimes I reward myself by hiding in my bed until the fist seizing my chest lets up. Ten minutes at a time. Sometimes ten seconds. That's how I live my life, surviving ten minutes at a time.

The story is done and sent to the author. I'll never make that mistake again. I'll never accept a story that sets my mind spinning with images of blood and guts. *Metal scraping against metal and the crunch of broken bones.* Never again. I must be more careful when I choose my work. I know how those kinds of stories upset me.

I had to shut the curtains and block out the street to force myself to work. Too often I find my attention shifting to the Masons' house. I saw him come back a few hours after he stormed out. He had the same duffel bag, but his hair appeared damp, as though he'd showered at a gym or pool. There wasn't any more shouting after he came back to the house, so I figured that they'd made up. Whatever they were arguing about, it sounded intense. I was actually surprised to see him return, I thought he'd gone for good. I was already wondering what would happen to the child. It's always the children who suffer in a divorce. I should know.

But no, the Mason husband came back, and I finished a difficult piece of work. For once, the Universe is throwing us a few bones on Cavendish Street. I find myself experiencing an emotion I've not felt for a while. Could it be hope? A smidgen of happiness? Whatever it is, I want to grasp it and clutch it tight in my fist, never letting go no matter how much it squirms around like a trapped bug. It's a warm day, and for once I feel the need for fresh air, so I put on a short sleeve top and leave the house for the co-op, with heady visions of the chocolate aisle playing on my mind.

I walk into the garden, lock the door, and make my way down the ginnel next to my house. All of these terraced streets have little alleyways that provide access to the back gardens. They are dark and grimy, but it's better than tramping the street into your living room carpet. I faff around with my shoulder bag while I'm walking, checking I have my keys and phone for the fiftieth time.

"Hello."

My head snaps up. It's her, Laura Mason, standing and waving to me from across the street. Her husband has his back to me, locking the front door. Their child, April, leans against the front of their house, fingering the string from her hoody.

"Hi," I reply, feeling my face warm with embarrassment. All I can think about is how I stood next to the window listening to their row. April had waved to me from across the street. She knows. She's a witness to my nosiness.

"I'm Laura," she says, offering me her hand to shake.

How I loathe our British customs. Why do we need to touch at all? Why do friends and family insist on a kiss on the cheek? Why hugs? I like my personal space, thank you very much. But I take her hand and limply shake. "Hannah."

"You're 73, right?" she says. "We moved in yesterday, so things are still a bit hectic. This is my husband, Matt, and our daughter, April."

I shake Matt's hand. It's huge, like a plumber's hands. More like a bear paw. He smiles with a lopsided grin, but all I can think about is how I can imagine his face growing red with rage, and using those hands as weapons. I try to block out the thoughts. I know nothing about this man. It's my imagination taking over again. It likes to do that. I glance back at Laura, who has on a yellow summer dress covered in large white polka dots, and her hair pulled back into a stylish bun. There are sunglasses pushed into her hair, expensive ones. She comes across like someone in complete control of everything.

"April, say hello to Hannah," Laura prompts.

April barely pulls her gaze from her hoody strings. "Hello." My eyes are drawn to her pale complexion and the dark eyes beneath her almost black hair. It could be my imagination, but I think I see red beneath her eyes. Perhaps the girl has been crying.

"She's shy," Laura says with a tight, apologetic smile.

"Nothing wrong with that," I say a little too brightly, the pity for the girl urging me to defend her. "I was shy too. Still am, really. All the best people are." I trail off, feeling my anxious urge to ramble taking over.

"Well, we're hoping the move might help her come out of her shell a little. Especially when she starts a new school."

Laura looks across at Matt and the two of them maintain a tense eye contact for a moment. Laura is the first to break it. There's tightness in the way she holds herself that makes me wonder if their row this morning is really over.

"Know anything about the schools round here?" Matt asks. "We're trying to make some decisions at the moment." He shoots Laura another hard glare and I begin to feel a little uncomfortable being around them both.

"No," I reply. "Sorry." My muscles clench as I wait for the inevitable question: *do you have children of your own*. But of course, it doesn't come. They've already seen that I live alone.

"I'm sorry, Hannah, we're holding you up. Are you on your way out somewhere? A spot of lunch, or a dinner date?"

I laugh. "No, nothing like that. I'm on my way up to the co-op." I cringe. "Not very glamorous, really." I know they must have seen that I rarely go out. They must think I'm so small and boring.

"Oh, that's where we're heading. Maybe we can walk with you?" Laura says, oblivious to my discomfort. "I'd love to know more about the area. How long have you lived here?"

We start to make our way up the hill and I feel the pull on my weak leg muscles. A little sweat breaks out on my forehead, but it's more like a cold sweat. I fold my arms around my chest as I consider their question. It's not something I want to think about. I never want to be reminded why I moved to Cavendish Street in the first place.

"Five years," I say. I rub the back of my hand across my face. "I hadn't realised it had been so long." Five years of this life. Five long years of only ever talking to Edith, of taking short trips to the co-op, of shopping online rather than in the city centre.

But has it been five years of that? Didn't I have more of a life to begin with? Even with everything that happened. Five years ago has been lost to me in a haze of another life. It's not tangible to me anymore. It'd may as well have happened to someone else.

"Oh well, you must know all the best places." Laura smiles, brightly. I'm envious of her ability to maintain that smile. Unlike my awkward self, she smooths over any bumps in conversation. But there are times when her smile is a bit frozen, or false. I shiver just thinking about what it's like in the Mason household when that smile is gone completely. "Are there any nice restaurants?"

I open and shut my mouth, trying to stall as I think as hard as I can. It's a normal question that any normal person could answer about the area they've lived in for five years, but I've never eaten out while living in Cavendish Street. Not even at a café for tea and a muffin. As I struggle to answer, the anxiety begins to build up again. *What if they realise I'm not normal? What if they see through me to what I really am?*

"I don't go out very often I'm afraid. I'm not the best person to ask."

"I saw a nice Italian down the road from the co-op," Matt says. "Al Forno, I think it was called. We'll have to check it out, babe." Matt reaches for Laura's waist, but she pulls away. She tries to cover it up with a girlish giggle but Matt's eyes become hard for a moment, and red flushes through his cheeks. He shakes his head and looks away.

"Oh," I say, trying to fill the awkward silence. "I forgot about that one. Yes, I think it's probably very nice."

Laura manoeuvres herself closer to me and further away from Matt. "I work such long hours that I never get the chance to go out anyway." She laughs, but there's little humour in it. "Poor Matt has to put up with me coming home at all hours."

"What do you do?" I ask.

"I work in finance," she replies, and there's a glimmer in her eye that tells me she doesn't really like working in finance and longs for a different life.

Knowing nothing about the financial sector, I decide not to probe further.

"What about you, Hannah?" Laura asks. It strikes me that she's a person who needs to know what everyone does for a living. I imagine that it's how she labels all the people she meets—important to unimportant, depending on their wage packet or status.

"I'm a freelance editor," I say, hearing the squeak of uncertainty in my voice. "So I work from home and get to read stories for a living. It's not so bad."

"Do you work with a publisher?" Laura asks, probably hoping for me to say, "why yes, I'm on the books with Harper Collins and Random Penguin, don't you know?". I could tell her about my Fiverr account, or my People-Per-Hour profile, but somehow it's not quite as impressive.

"No, I work mainly with independent publishers and authors," I reply.

She nods, and a small, wry smile passes over her lips, as though I've just confirmed an opinion for her. A bristle works its way through my body as I realise I'm being judged. I know that my life is lame, but that doesn't mean I want someone judging me about it.

"How exciting," she says.

"Oh, not really." I know she's humouring me, and she

knows she's humouring me. Maybe she's one of those people who grew up with really interesting parents that hung around with the London creative scene. Her accent sounds Southern. I bet she went to fondue parties as a kid and shook hands with Nobel prize winners. I shake the thought away. There goes my imagination again.

"Well, Hannah, I think we're the only women around our age on the street. Everyone else is at least twenty years older." She tips her head back to laugh.

"You've met Edith then?" I say, trying to sound funny and normal.

She rolls her eyes. "Yes. She told us all about Derek."

All thought of humour dissipates. I'm left with a cold, clammy feeling over my skin. "She did?"

"Yes, what a tragedy," Laura says.

"What's this?" Matt interrupts.

"I'll tell you later," Laura replies. She moves her head towards April in a fast motion as though trying to convey to Matt "not in front of the kid".

But Matt either ignores or fails to notice Laura's signal. "Tell me now." His back straightens and his bulging arms fold across his wide chest, making him appear even larger than before.

"Matt." Laura's voice is stern and between gritted teeth. I look away, embarrassed. "Not in front of April." She lowers her voice. "An old man died. In our house."

I'm uncomfortable, and it makes the anxiety spread through me. Gone is that feeling of accomplishment that I managed to get out of the house, that I'm having a good day. Now waves of sickness and panic are taking me over, and I'm forced to use all my willpower on keeping a straight face. *Get through the next ten seconds. Seem like you're normal. Don't grimace. Now the next ten seconds. You won't be sick. You won't faint. It's in your head.*

"What?" Matt is louder than his wife. "Why didn't you tell me? Where?"

"Where what, Matt?" Laura says, her eyes flashing furiously. "Let's not talk about this now. Hannah, seeing as we're pretty much the only two women on the street younger than fifty, do you fancy meeting for a glass of wine every now and then? I could pop round to yours with a bottle if you like."

Matt's lips pull into a thin line, making me think that he doesn't approve of this idea one little bit. But I feel too cornered to do anything but smile, nod, and say that it sounds like a lovely idea. I'm digging deep for more to say when a strange sense of silence washes over the street. And in that moment, April whips around and stops dead on the pavement. Her eyes are wide and ringed with red. For the first time, I realise how extraordinarily pale her skin is, and how paper-thin delicate the texture appears. There are fine hairs over her cheeks that catch the afternoon sun, making her glow. Looking at her delivers a punch to my gut, so hard that I could double over, but I force myself not to. She's so young, and so beautiful, *and everything I could have had.*

Then she opens her mouth, and she screams.

LAURA

It happened on the street and everyone turned to stare. It took us at least five minutes to calm her down, during which Hannah made her excuses and scuttled home without even going to the shops. Now Matt isn't talking to me, because he says I was too hard on her. I didn't *do* anything, I just told her to pull herself together. There were people staring at us for God's sake. One old woman—who looked a lot like one of Edith's friends—came over and started asking if she was all right.

"The more attention you give her, the more she'll do it," I hiss, as I grab hold of a trolley and dump my bag in it. April is lagging behind us, dragging her feet along, still sniffling. "You know that's why she does it."

Matt moves closer to me, invading my space with his bulk. He leans towards me and I cringe away. "Do I? Or maybe, just maybe, she needs some help, Laura. This is why I want to send her to private school."

I make a disgusted sound. "Don't try to emotionally

blackmail me. Comprehensive schools can be just as good at dealing with behavioural problems—"

"Oh really?" he raises his voice.

There are people in the co-op gawking at us now. We've barely even made it inside before we stop to argue with each other in hushed tones that aren't really fooling anyone.

"You can't think for even a second that she would be better off somewhere that specialises in helping kids like her?" Matt says, getting gradually louder. "You are so fucking selfish sometimes."

"*I'm* selfish? You only want her to go to private school because you're a snob." I start pushing the trolley away. "Have you forgotten where *you* came from—"

"That's exactly why I want a different life for her. Don't you see that?"

"You want the status, that's what you want. And you want a life we can't afford, that you can't even pay for. *I'm* the one paying for everything, because you can't be arsed to go out and get a job."

Matt's eyes rage, but he shuts his mouth with an audible snap of his teeth. I've gone too far, I can feel it. My daughter walks along with her hands over her ears and tears prick at my eyes. I cover my mouth to smother a sob, and realise that my hands are shaking. What have I done?

"April, would you like some chocolate, sweetheart? You can have whatever you like," I say.

She shakes her head, still covering her ears. Matt has his back to me, but the rest of the shop has turned to watch us, even the cashier women.

"Matt, get her some of those chocolate stars she likes." I place a hand on his shoulder, but it's as hard as a rock, and as unyielding, too. I'm dangerously close to bursting into tears inside the co-op. "I'm sorry."

But Matt shrugs me away and walks off. I take hold of April's hand, and follow him, pulling my daughter along behind me. What has happened to my family?

HANNAH

"She stood there screaming in the street." Edith attacks an unruly dandelion weed with her trowel. "Then they had a right old barney in the co-op. Alice saw it all. She said it was really strange. That girl just stood there, pale and skinny, screeching like a banshee. She said she'd never seen owt like it." The dandelion comes up, but the root snaps in half, so Edith bends lower, scraping at the remainder of the weed. Her voice becomes strained with the effort, and I hear the phlegm building up in her chest. "Kids these days don't know they're born. My older sister saw all sorts during the war, and do you know what she did?" She looks up, waiting for me to respond. I shake my head. "She put up and shut up. Never talked about it, she didn't. She was just a kid. Me dad, well, he never spoke about it. Mum said he didn't come back right, but he never spoke about it."

I stare hard at the wine glass in my hand. "People still go through things they don't talk about."

"Aye, but nowt like that."

I feel like pointing out that there are still wars around the world, but decide it's best not to even bother. Despite being born a year or two before WW2 ended, Edith has a habit of telling everyone she meets that because they didn't live through the war, they "don't know they're born" without even recognising the irony.

"But then we don't know what goes on, do we?" she continues. The last of the root is emerging from the soil, now. "I mean, the fella seems a bit of a wild one. He had another car outside the house yesterday. Spent all day revving it, he did. I wish he'd put his shirt on, for crying out loud." She chucks the last of the root onto her weeding pile and straightens her back. "Pass us that glass of water would you, love." She pulls off her gardening gloves and wipes a slick of sweat from her forehead. I pick up the water from the small outdoor table set up close to the house, and travel the few steps across to the flower bed. "You know, it's good exercise this. You should try it sometime." Her old blue eyes flicker with a combination of mischief and dislike. Edith likes to gossip, so she'll talk to anyone, but I don't think she actually likes me.

"Oh, I've not got green fingers. I even killed that spider plant you gave me." I climb back onto my step and take another sip from the glass of wine, feeling the alcohol soothe the anxiety that's forming somewhere deep inside my body. I can understand how people become alcoholics. I've found myself slipping that way a few times. But I treat it like I do my panic. *Stop. Deep breath. Get through the next ten minutes without a drink. Then the next.* And somehow, I've managed to keep my drinking as a recreation, and not a prerequisite.

Edith tuts. "Well, I suppose it's not for everyone." She

coughs, then sips more of her water. "Have you seen much of the Masons?"

I choose a spot on my knee to run my finger around, feeling the circular motion through my leggings. It gives me precious seconds to decide how much to say. I don't want to tell her that I was there when April started screaming, or how I woke up hearing that same scream ringing in my ears last night. Nor do I want to tell her that I've been watching the Masons over the last week, observing that April wanders away from the house on her own during the day, and overhearing some of Matt and Laura's arguments either late at night or early in the mornings. Neither will I say that I keep seeing Matt Mason leave April alone in the middle of the day as he disappears with a duffel bag. Sometimes he's gone for most of the day, only returning in the late afternoon. I don't want Edith spreading this knowledge around the street, but more than that, I don't want to share this information with anyone. It feels too personal, not to the Masons, but to me. They have become more than the neighbours across the street. They've become almost an obsession.

"Not much," I say. "I've seen them to say hello to."

"Well, I heard shouting coming from that house the other day. Old Peter next to them is too deaf to hear owt, and the Akbars on the other side never speak to me. I doubt they can even speak English." She rolls her eyes and I bite my tongue. Then she hobbles over to me and sits down in the deck chair on her side of the garden, close to the table I retrieved her water from. "But do you know the woman comes home at all hours? She's never there to cook tea for them. The husband takes care of the kid all day. That's an odd set up."

I suppress the urge to roll my eyes. Edith, along with

much of the world, sees the woman's role as little more than a mother and a housekeeper (unless a war is on of course).

"Maybe it works for them," I offer.

She shakes her head. "If it was working, they wouldn't be fighting at all hours, traumatising the child, would they? I bet that's why the kid is acting up, you know, because of all the disruptions. And he's not much better, disappearing in the middle of the day."

I turn to Edith. She'd noticed it too. So it wasn't my imagination. "I think he goes to the gym a lot."

"Yes, but, he doesn't always take his bag with him. I don't know much about these gyms, but I do know people need to change out of their mucky clothes afterward." Her eyes are sparkling, excited by the gossip. Turned on by the mystery. "It's odd to leave that kid alone for so long. Mind, thirteen is plenty big enough to look after yourself. I could cook a roast dinner by the age of twelve and use me mum's sewing machine. But it's not right for a man not to have a proper job. He should be out of the house all day, grafting, not tinkering with his car and bobbing off to God knows where. It can't be a job, can it? He leaves at different times, sometimes he's gone an hour, sometimes it's five. Besides, I asked her summat, you know, Laura Mason. I asked her if he had a job and she said he was between clients or some such nonsense. Nah, you could tell that he didn't have a job from the expression on her face. She was embarrassed, it was plain as day." She pops a cigarette into her mouth and flicks open her lighter. Before she lights the fag, she says, "But where does he go? That's what I want to know."

LAURA

Even in midsummer I'm driving home in the dark. There was an accident in the city centre, making coming out of Sheffield a complete nightmare. Trying to get back to my new suburban home is taking forever. I hadn't wanted to move so far away from my job, but sometimes life takes us places we don't expect. This isn't the worst hardship in the world, I just need to knuckle down and get on with it.

The night air is muggy enough for me to keep my car window open and to drive without my jacket on. Instead, I'm in a flimsy blouse that sticks to my skin. There was an issue at work today. Two accountants messed up, and I had to speak to the board about their mistake. As the manager, the responsibility rests on me to get everything right, even though it was those arseholes who fucked up the numbers, not me. When a red Skoda pulls out in front of me, my hand reaches for the horn, but I stop myself. Instead, I lean back against the headrest and drum my fingernails against the steering wheel.

Matt will be furious when I get in. I've been dodging his

calls, knowing that he'll want me to come home early so I can have tea with him and April. I sent him a text about an hour ago. *Mental day at work. Leaving now and will be home soon.* But I left twenty minutes after I sent the message, and then got stuck in traffic. That wasn't supposed to happen. The streets are usually dead by the time I drive home.

But I have to admit to myself that it was at least in part a conscious decision. I'm avoiding home. I'm avoiding the rows, and the shouting. I want to keep away from Matt's temper, which is forever boiling over right now. I'm avoiding April's strange, elusive behaviour, and the fact that she never seems to leave her bedroom. Sometimes, when I'm driving home, I wonder what it would be like to take a different direction and keep driving until I find somewhere I want to stop. What would it be like to start all over again? To be on my own? Once, while I was thinking about this, I accidentally drove to our old house. There, in the window, sat a new family, eating in the dining room like we used to. Now we never eat together. I work overtime. I work weekends. I take on as much as I can, and it's not only for the flexi-time, it's because *I don't want to go home.*

But with that realisation comes the guilt. How can I be a mother and even think that? How can I let that thought drift into my mind? I'm a terrible person. As I finally reach my turning to get out of the city, I start to think about what I can afford to buy April at the weekend. Some new clothes, perhaps? We could go shopping together. Maybe a new notebook, one of those fancy ones with a leather cover. She likes to write. Or some new pens. I know now not to buy April the kind of stuff that other kids her age love—like expensive trainers, or games consoles. She never uses them. Matt plays on the new Xbox, April hardly touches it. Sometimes he manages to persuade her to play games with him, but even then she shows little interest. She doesn't even try to win.

I find myself slowing down as I come out of the city. I guess I'm putting off the inevitable. But the thing is, I can't work out how many of my worries are in my head, and how many are genuine. Has April really got a serious problem, or am I making too much of it? The screaming in public is the worst, but maybe it's attention seeking. She's always been the kind of kid who wanted all the attention, but then didn't know what to do with it when she had it. A sort of insecure neediness.

And Matt, maybe it's all the stress of being unemployed. Sometimes I think he's self-sabotaging, that he's the only one stopping himself becoming a personal trainer. He's so frightened of failing that he can't even start. Maybe, just maybe, all these problems are fixable.

I manoeuvre onto the street before Cavendish Street, where the woods back onto the road. It's a quiet street with only a few street lamps and a field separating the road from a thicket of trees. Matt tried to sell me the house based on these woods alone—we could get a dog and go for family walks together. He could jog through the woods in the mornings when the sun was rising. I'd agreed and made all the enthusiastic noises that he needed to hear, but secretly, the place gave me the creeps. I've never liked woods, not since I was a child.

It's almost a relief to pull onto Cavendish. There's a tickle in my tummy, a butterflies feeling, about going home. It's not a pleasant sensation, like when you expect something good to happen, it's more of a warning. I pull up on the side of the street—on-road parking is a pain in the arse—and turn the key. No matter how much I try to tell myself that all my problems can be fixed, I can't stop the tension working its way through my muscles at the thought of going inside the house. I take a deep breath before opening the car door and making my way into the house.

Matt is standing in the kitchen with his arms folded across his chest. I try not to make eye contact as I fiddle with the door, and then spend a few moments messing with my jacket and shoes.

"Sorry love," I say, realising my voice is too high. "There was an accident in town. I got caught in traffic. Oh and I had to speak to the board because of an almighty cock-up. I was in a meeting with them for three hours if you can believe it. I'm knackered."

Finally I meet his eyes. My throat goes dry. His expression is cold. His jaw is clamped tight, and there's a bulging vein along his temple.

"I'm sorry, babe." I reach out to touch him, but he flings his arm out, smacking my hand away. I let out a little cry and rub the sore spot on the back of my hand.

"I made pasta," he says. "You can heat it up if you want."

He storms out of the kitchen, and I hear the sound of the TV switching onto the sports channel. I find a Tupperware box of pasta and put it in the microwave.

How did it all change? How did we end up like this? I remember when Matt would cook special meals for us, scallop risotto, lamb shank, sea bass... and I would rush home from work so I could spend time with him. He was a different person then. Or at least I thought he was. His desire for the best always felt like desire for the best for me, not him. Now I feel like an ornament or a gadget that's supposed to fit into his perfect idea of a life: an uncontrollable object that he desperately wants to control.

The microwave pings. I unload it onto a plate and take it into the living room to eat on my lap.

"What are you doing?" he asks, gesturing to the plate in my hand.

"I've come to eat," I reply.

"You're not eating in here. Eat at the table in the kitchen." He turns away from me. His voice is devoid of all emotion.

"Are you kidding? It's late, Matt. I'm not playing games."

"It's the rule of the house," he says. "Eat at the table."

"I'm not sitting on my own eating my dinner. Grow the fuck up."

He's on his feet. "Then I'll come with you."

From the challenge in his eyes, I know this is a game he wants to win. He wants the control back.

"Fine."

I eat in silence, with Matt's eyes watching me the entire time. I daren't speak. I'm too tired for an argument. It's too hot, too sticky and claustrophobic in this house for that tonight. The open windows let nothing but stale air into the house.

Matt at least appears to relax as he watches me eat. A petty part of me urges to throw the plate across the room, or to storm out of the house, but I don't. I let him have it.

"That wasn't so hard was it?" he says, taking my plate to wash.

"Sorry you missed your football game," I say, glad the ordeal is over.

"Highlights," he says. "Nothing important."

"Did you have a good day?" The small talk should be

natural. We should be natural, but we aren't. We're stilted and wrong, like jigsaw pieces forced into the wrong position.

Matt shrugs. "I went for a walk with April. I think she's getting used to the area slowly but surely. You know how cautious she is about change."

I nod. "Well done for getting her out of the house. That's more than I can manage."

He rinses the plate under the tap. I should probably offer my help, but I don't want to ruin this moment we have, so I stay quiet.

"I like spending time with her. You really need to get some one-on-one time with her, Lors, you're really missing out. I have all this time in the day where it's just us, you know? You don't get any of that."

I chew on my bottom lip, resenting the reminder. "I'll take her shopping this weekend. We'll go to Meadowhall and get Pizza Express."

"She doesn't eat pizza anymore."

"What? Why?"

"She wants to be healthier," Matt replies. "It wouldn't hurt us all to eat a little better."

I prickle, resenting his words. "I guess so."

I start to make my way back into the living room but Matt's arms snake around my middle. I immediately tense up, and that makes him hold me tighter. Then his mouth is on my neck, pushing my hair away, tasting my skin.

"Matt," I say with laughter in my voice. "I'm still gross from the drive here."

"We'll shower together," he murmurs into my neck.

"I'm tired."

"Shh, you're not."

His arms are constricting me, like a vice, slowly squeezing the life from me. I try to squirm out of his grip, but he's too strong.

"Matt," I say, this time with a warning tone in my voice, slightly high with panic. "I'm serious."

He sighs and lets me go, pushing past me into the living room. I pull my hair back into place and head upstairs. The air here is stifling, so I open the window in our bedroom. I prowl around our room for a few moments, trying to force nervous energy bouncing around my body to be still. It's no use, I'm too on edge.

I step out onto the landing and walk across to April's room. The door is shut, and the light is off. April is a light sleeper, so I decide not to pop my head in to see her, even though I badly want to.

Instead, I start delving into the laundry basket, separating light and dark items, in some desperate need for my body to move. A sheen of sweat forms on my forehead as I work, but I ignore the heat and the frantic nature of my hands. I ignore my thoughts, fractured and worrying. Is my marriage irreparable? Does April hate me?

When I check the pockets of Matt's jeans for tissues—the man is terrible for leaving them in all of his trousers—my fingers find a screwed up piece of paper. I'm about to throw it out when I decide to open it up instead.

"The bastard!"

My temper is quick to flare when I feel I've been wronged. I'm a hater of the unfair, but most of all I hate a liar. I hurry downstairs with the receipt held out between two fingers.

"What the fuck is this? Who is she? Who are you screwing?"

Matt stares up at me from the sofa with his mouth agape. He has such a slack face. It's an unwrinkled, unintelligent face.

"What are you talking about?"

I throw the receipt towards him and it flutters through the air, forcing him to snatch it before it floats down to the carpet.

"It's a receipt, Laura. Can't you read?"

I'm shaking with anger. "A receipt for two lunches in a fancy restaurant that you paid for."

Matt is on his feet. "You think I'm having an affair because of one receipt?"

"Well something is going on," I say. "You've been secretive and argumentative—"

"Since when have I been secretive? I'll tell you all about it shall I? I met up with a potential client about a job."

I roll my eyes. "Oh, pull the other one. You've not had any clients for months."

Matt's face goes red and the vein is bulging over his temple again. He throws the receipt onto the sofa and covers the space between us.

"You're my wife, Laura. You're my fucking wife, and this is what I get? I get accused of cheating, and ridiculed in the same day? You work so late I never see you. In fact, yeah, I'm sure of it, you're avoiding me and April. You could be the one having an affair not me."

"Don't be stupid."

Matt grabs my face. "I'm not stupid, I'm not ridiculous, I'm your husband." He pushes me up against the wall. His mouth presses against mine.

HANNAH

When I wake, my arms fly up in front of my face. *The glass*, I think. *It's all my fault.* The suffocating guilt comes back, so hard and fast that it's like a kick to the abdomen. But there's nothing here, only a stuffy dark room and a sweat soaked bed. I lift up my knees and push my face into them, feeling the perspiration from my forehead seep into my leggings.

The window is wide open, but the curtains are shut, keeping the air from travelling in or out. I turn over and seek out my mobile phone from within a crevice between the pillows and disconnect it from my charger. It's only just past midnight. I've been asleep for maybe an hour. I tip my head back and sigh, wondering when I last had a decent night's sleep. I flinch, because I remember exactly when that was, and I hadn't been alone.

If I had been even remotely sleepy, the raised voices coming from across the street would have killed it once and for all. I pad across the bedroom floor and slowly open the curtains. There's a faint glow coming from inside number 72.

They're fighting again, with muffled voices that leave the subject of their argument inaccessible. I move away. I shouldn't be spying on them. I should leave them alone and live my own life.

I can't help but laugh at myself. *My own life.* What is that? The four walls of my house? The walk to the co-op and back? The treadmill that never gets used? Feeling angry now —with myself, with the Masons for waking me up, and with my circumstances—I grab my laptop from my bedside table and start checking my emails for new work. I have five more orders. Two of which I'll have to reject because they contain violence. No matter how many times I tell people I won't accept violent stories, I still get them appearing in my inbox. People always think they are the exception: *my story is violent, but it's so good she won't notice; everyone else's child is a brat, but mine is an angel; the sign says no smoking, but I really need one.* No one likes to be ordinary. Everyone wants to be different. People try so hard to be different, that they end up all being the same. Just like me, with my working from home attitude, my "I'm independent and don't need anyone" approach. What a joke that is.

My parents passed away seven years ago and I drifted away from friends when I moved to Cavendish Street, but my brother James was concerned about me for a while. He thought I was hiding away; from the world, from my past. I'm running without going anywhere, stuck on life's dusty treadmill. My brother was the one who was always right. He always guessed the culprit when we watched *Midsomer Murders* and *Poirot* together. And he was always smug about it, pointing out the murderer in the first ten minutes as we huddled under the duvet watching the old TV/VCR combo while Mum and

Dad argued downstairs. We were uncool kids, although he got cooler as he moved into his mid-teens. I didn't. And as he fell in with the popular crowd, his smugness became more and more irritating. While my geekiness, my propensity for escaping into fantasy fiction and films, became more and more lame.

Maybe that's why we don't call each other anymore.

I give up pretending to work. I open Facebook and type Matthew Mason into the search bar. As my fingers move along the keyboard, I get a delicious feeling of mischief that I haven't had since James and I created the "terrible two" club in our shed, designed to fight crime and solve mysteries. I was ten, James was twelve. We didn't solve anything, but we did eat a lot of Liquorice All-Sorts and read The Beano.

There are a few Matthew Masons. The first two are older, with beards. There's a young guy pouting, with bleach blond hair and an orange tan. Then, about five down, I see him. I almost skipped straight passed him, because the profile picture makes him appear far younger than he really is. I click on it and go through to his Facebook page, which is set to private with a few public photographs.

His profile picture is a selfie taken in the mirror. It's one of those photos where the camera flash obscures some of the person, and casts the rest of the room into darkness. It's possible that Matt has used some sort of retro filter on top, because everything appears unnaturally washed out, like an Instagram picture. My top lip curls up. It's such a try-hard photograph. His pose is awkward. He's clearly trying to emulate the kind of selfies posted by lads half his age, with his arms sticking out to emphasise his bulky muscles, and his gaze not meeting the camera. He comes across as vain and cocky, not someone I would ever find attractive.

When I click on the picture, it shows all the likes and comments from his friends. Most of the comments are from women, or more specifically, girls. They can't be much older than twenty, these girls. I actually make a disgusted noise in my throat when I read them: *looking hot. Hellooooo bicep.* This guy has a wife and a daughter and he's friends with all these girls? I poke around on his page some more. In the "about me" section it says that he's a personal trainer. I think back to my conversation with Edith. I guess his job could explain where he goes, although Laura told Edith that he was between clients right now. But, seriously, does he only train with twenty-year-old girls? Most of them are probably at uni and can't afford a personal trainer, unless the world has changed that much since I was a student. I lived on baked beans and noodles for the three years.

I move the pointer back to the search bar and type in Laura Mason. Unlike her husband's, her profile picture is easy to spot. There she is, result two, smiling at the camera in a smart-casual blazer with tasteful make-up and straightened hair. She resembles one of those solicitors on an accident claim advertisement. Everything about her picture says "I'm approachable, but also professional". I already find myself approving of Laura and the way she puts herself across on the internet. Her page is public, but it's more like a professional advert than anything personal. She rarely posts, and when she does, her posts are motivational quotes about business and work. After a few moments of poking around, I'm bored.

I get up off the bed and walk over to the window. The shouting has stopped, but another noise is coming from across the road. I listen more carefully. The sound is grunting. My cheeks flush with embarrassment when I realise they are sex noises. I'm listening to Matt and Laura have sex. God, not only have I stalked them on Facebook, but I've also listened to them having sex. I reach across to draw the curtains when movement across the street distracts me. It's April's room. Her light has been switched on. I could swear that I saw her move.

I feel sick to the stomach. I pull the curtains back, blocking out the view of the street. As I walk back towards my bed, I touch my stomach lightly. It's churning, unrestful, like my body is anticipating an awful event, but my mind can't think what it could be.

They've made up again. First they were shouting, then everything went quiet, and now I can hear kissing and mumbling. I put my headphones on and turned the music up. I don't want to hear that. I've been writing in my diary, it's the one thing I like to do. I don't like talking so much. Mum is always on at me about making more friends. She's obsessed with it. But what's so wrong with wanting to write and draw and listen to music?

I lift up one side of my headphones and shudder at what I hear. How am I supposed to go back to sleep now? Not that I sleep properly anyway, not when I know he is in the house.

HANNAH

The next morning, I have that hangover feeling from not getting enough sleep. I even have that sense of regret, that feeling that I did something bad. I'm a little ashamed about internet stalking the Masons last night. But deep down, I know I haven't let it go. I'm still so curious that I leave my living room window wide open, and sit on my sofa with a cup of tea, no TV on, listening. Maybe I'll hear them arguing again.

Laura Mason leaves for work at 7:30am. She's wearing a grey skirt suit and high heels. Her hair is pulled back into a tight bun, and her make-up is subtle. I don't get a good view of her face, but it appears to be a little more swollen than usual. It could be the early morning, it could be from crying, or it could be any number of things, including my imagination. It's nothing concrete that I can build my suspicions on.

I have to think about this rationally—which is difficult when you've been living in the opposite of logic and reason for so long. What do I really suspect is going on with the Masons? First, Matt Mason strikes me as the typical alpha male dirtbag who likes to control and manipulate women. But, the counter argument to that suspicion is that Laura Mason gives the impression of independence and strength. She didn't mind standing up to Matt when we were walking to the co-op. She did nothing to make me believe she was frightened of him. She doesn't have the air of a meek, battered woman at all.

Second, their daughter April is quiet and subdued. I think back to her screaming in the middle of the street, and the panic rises in my chest again. No child should ever scream like that. It had pierced through the air and echoed around the street. My skin crawls as I think about it. What makes a child scream like that? Could it have all been for attention? Or is there something else going on? Maybe it's this strange maternal urge to protect her that's clouding my judgement, but my gut tells me that April is in trouble.

A mother who spends all her time at work. Parents who fight. A father who's immature and vain. It's like a pot getting ready to boil over. I didn't save Derek when he died right in front of my nose. Maybe I can stop whatever might happen to April.

After Laura leaves, Matt comes out and begins tinkering around with his car. I pretend to be typing on my laptop, but really I'm watching the road. April is there. She sits on the kerb, with her head low. Sometimes she takes out a small book from her pocket and scribbles a few notes inside. Other times, Matt orders her around, getting her to fetch him tools or cups of tea. April doesn't smile a lot, even when Matt jokes around with her. Sometimes he ruffles her hair and she moves away, as though flinching. Unless it's my wandering imagination...

"What's the matter, A?" I hear Matt say.

I move closer to the window, pretending to be dusting or tidying so I don't raise any suspicions.

"Are you in a mood or summat?"

April shrugs.

"Women," Matt says with a shake of his head. He gives her this huge smile, which doesn't reach his eyes. He smiles like that a lot. All of the Masons have mastered the art of the fake smile. "You're all the same. Rag week is it?"

April gazes up at him now. Her eyes flash with emotion, but I'm too far away to tell what it is. Anger? Fear? She gets to her feet, shoves her hands in her pockets and scuttles quickly back into the home.

Matt throws his spanner down and it clatters loudly against the pavement. "Fucking kids."

His burst of anger makes me start. I move away from the window, trying to angle my body so I can see between the curtains, but remain out of sight. Matt is collecting his tools and shoving them into a bag. He slams the bonnet of his car and locks the car door. Then he disappears into the house, wiping the grime from his hands onto his jeans.

Laura and Matt could not be more different from each other. She's so prim and proper, him so rough and rude. I can't help but wonder why these people are together in the first place, and why they thought it was a good idea to bring a child into their mess. People can be so selfish. They think children will fix all their problems, when in fact they're bringing more lives into an already messy situation. I should know. I've lived it. I've been the pawn in their little games. I know exactly what it's like.

For some reason, I feel uncomfortable knowing that Matt

and April are alone in the house together. I shake my head. He's her father, for God's sake. What am I thinking?

I'm about to move away and force myself to get on with my own life, when Matt comes out of the house in fresh clothes. He locks the door, and starts off up the street. My heartbeat quickens. I know what I should do. I should mind my own business. But all I can think about is Edith saying to me in her smoker's rasp: *where does he go?* Because it's weird for a dad to leave his young daughter alone so often. It's weird. And, yeah, I know she's thirteen and that's old enough to be home alone for a few hours, but it's still an odd thing to do.

Before I know it, I'm slipping my feet into shoes and grabbing my bag. I leave through the back door and hurry along the alleyway. My pulse is racing, and I'm filled with an exhilaration that feels different to the usual creeping anxiety that builds through my body. For once I have a plan. I have a desire to leave this stale house and go out into the open air. It feels strange to have a goal.

So I can't screw it up. If I'm going to let myself go this far, I have to do it for a reason. I have to commit.

It's getting on for midday, and it's another hot morning. I hadn't even checked what I was wearing before leaving the house, but I glance down now, and remember that I pulled on my white skirt and red T-shirt. It could be worse. I generally lounge around in sportswear, but it was too hot for jogging bottoms today.

I quicken my pace so that I find Matt ahead of me. He's walking with purpose, his hips and shoulders swinging as he walks. I, on the other hand, walk with stiff, short steps. I fold my arms across my chest as though trying to protect myself. I keep pushing hair away from my face like a nervous twitch. I guess I'm not usually aware of my ticks, but now, as I can't help but think about what I look like and whether I stand out, I can't stop noticing them. I change my speed several times, trying to seem like I'm just out for a stroll, but also keeping up with Matt. There's no point trying to hide behind corners or in shadows. It's so strikingly bright that there's nowhere to hide. Luckily, Matt's concentration is not directed at me, but the street ahead. I'm safe from suspicion. For now.

We pass the co-op and continue down the main shopping street. Our suburb is tiny, and there isn't much here—a butcher who sells more second hand DVDs than meat, a liquor store, a newsagent, a church—then Matt takes a right.

I'm following along behind him, taking the same turning he does. My heart is thumping now, and it's not just because I'm stalking someone so I can snoop on their private life, it's because this is the furthest I've been from my home in a long time. I brush the hair from my face, then bite my thumbnail. This street is more residential, but there is a pub on the corner that I'd never noticed before. From the outside it has the appearance of the kind of place filled with alcoholics and men who still complain about the smoking ban. The sign says "The Dog and Partridge" and has a faded painting on the front and back. It swings on squeaky hinges above a door with peeling paint. My stomach drops when Matt walks into the pub.

I've not set foot in a pub for years. The thought makes me feel physically sick. All those people, all that noise. But I can't go back now. I have to go in. I pull my phone out of my skirt pocket and check the time. It's five minutes past midday. The pub will have opened a few minutes ago. There's no way it'll be busy now. Matt could see me in there, and then what would be my excuse? That I wanted a drink at this time? I notice the chalkboard advertising their sandwich menu. I can say I popped in for lunch. That's a normal thing for a person who works from home to do. Not that I know a lot about being normal.

I can't go back now. I swing open the door with an arm that feels double its weight, and fight my way through the fog of anxiety. There's music on, a cheesy pop song from the sixties I think. Maybe a one hit wonder or a chart-topping pop tune. The woman behind the bar is singing along as she wipes a rag down the bar. She must be over fifty, and has one of those pursed mouths with deep wrinkles that smokers get. She nods and smiles at me, her eyes large behind thick lensed glasses.

"What can I get you, love?"

I'm already embarrassed by my lack of Yorkshire accent, and I have to check my pocket to reassure myself that I brought my purse with me, although I'm not sure how much cash I actually have. But I answer in a quiet voice, "A Coke please," before scanning the room, checking for Matt Mason. He's not here, but I can see a doorway to another room.

"That's the dining area. Are you after lunch?" the woman asks. She plonks my Coke on the counter and lifts her chin. "One fifty."

"Um, no thanks," I say handing her the cash. "Just the drink for now."

"Right you are, love. I'm here if you change your mind."

I move away from the bar and find a table close to the restaurant entrance. My stomach lurches when I see the back of Matt Mason's head, but I tell myself to stay calm and not do anything to attract attention to myself, like gawping over at his table. So I set down my Coke and settle into my seat, pretending that my phone is really interesting. When I finally allow myself to look at his table, I see that Matt is not alone. He's with a woman.

It takes me five minutes of ignoring the sweat forming on my forehead and the panic rising in my chest, to get a good view of her features through what I hope are subtle glances. She's young, too young. She could be a first year University student, dressed in that "couldn't-give-a-toss" kind of way most students prefer. It's the "just rolled out of bed and pulled on the first clothes available" style. Her apparel consists of joggers and a strappy top. Most of the girls from the University dress like that, with their hair pulled up into a messy top knot. Their eyeliner smudged down to their cheeks, and they're always in knock-off Uggs.

This girl wears the same kind of clothes, but she's not wearing make-up at all. She doesn't need to. She's exception-ally pretty and a true English rose, with almost black hair, and peachy skin. She stares at Matt as though he's saying some-thing really interesting, occasionally reaching over to touch his hand. Their conversation appears animated and relaxed. I see the girl tip her head back to laugh a few times. Then she strokes his face, leaning in to kiss him.

A hard lump forms in my chest. I can't help thinking of Laura—prim and proper Laura—who means well, even if she isn't the warmest person. She's at work right now, assuming that her husband is doing his bit in their partnership by caring for their child. Instead, he's out with this teenager, kissing her in public. I cut off that thought. I'm angry with Matt because of what I've seen, but maybe I'm jumping to too many conclusions. I don't have any proof that he doesn't care for April. All I know is that he's a cheating scum-bag. I can't keep letting my imagination get the better of me. One of these days it's going to take over completely.

"Want some company, sweetheart?"

I pulled away from Matt Mason and his mistress to find a swaying man leering at me. He leans down towards my table, so that I can smell the beer on his breath, and see his yellowing teeth. He must be well past fifty, and has an unpleasant smattering of grey stubble on his chin. I lean away from him, gripping the edge of the table acting as a barrier between us.

"No thank you," I say.

"Leave her alone you drunken old git," the barmaid shouts. She shoos the man away with her cloth, and he stumbles away grumbling.

But the damage is done. That hard lump explodes in my chest, finally letting out all the anxiety that has been building since I left the house. I get shakily to my feet, but I'm struggling to breathe and my mind is racing. If I stay, the drunk man might not leave me alone. He might try to touch or kiss me. He might follow me home and hurt me. I have to get out of this place, but my legs are wobbling beneath me and I feel like I might throw up. The thought of vomiting in public makes it even harder for me to breathe.

Get through the next ten seconds.

Behind me, there's the sound of broken glass and an image flashes across my mind.

Broken bones. The glass. It was all my fault.

"Are you all right, love?"

The words come to me as though through water. My ears are thumping with the sound of my pulse, and the pub drifts in and out of focus. The woman with the glasses is staring at me with her huge bug eyes and I have to get out of that place. There's movement from the restaurant. I guess I've made a scene and now Matt and his mistress are about to come out to see what the commotion is. I have to get out of this place. Finally, my legs start to work. I push past the woman, desperate for fresh air. I run out of the pub.

HANNAH

I barely make it through the door before I throw up. My head is swimming with things I want to forget, but I can't seem to block them out. I rush through into the living room and open the window to let out the stench of vomit. I need to calm down, but my heart is racing. I stagger back to the kitchen and run the cold tap, splashing my face and neck with water.

Get through the next ten seconds.

What was I thinking? I'm too messed up to start involving myself in other people's problems. I'm hanging on by a thread, haunted by events I'd rather forget.

Get through the next ten seconds.

Stop thinking about it. I force my mind to shut down. My body is still full of nervous energy, so I grab a cup and fill it with water.

Get through the next ten seconds.

The water helps to soothe the panic. I sip it slowly, relishing how it slips down my throat. The tension in my chest begins to dissipate. I'm at home. It's safe here. I can get through this.

During my second glass of water I start to feel better. But I still have to worry about Matt Mason, and the way I followed him to that pub. What if he saw me? I know his secret now. Does that put me in danger? I could ruin his marriage, ruin him. I run my fingers through my damp hair and start pacing the length of the kitchen. I should tell Laura about what I saw, but I don't know her, and I don't know Matt, and I don't know how either of them are going to react. I don't know if it's even safe to do so.

I shake my head, and get the bottle of vodka out from the fridge, pouring myself two fingers into the same mug I drank water from. The time for water is over. I need a stiff drink. I need to decide what to do.

But instead of deciding, I clean up the sick by the door, wincing at the smell. By the time I'm done, my hands have stopped shaking and I can breathe again. I take another sip of vodka, enjoying the heat. Even though I had a terrible panic attack, I went outside and I talked to someone, and I even had a drink in a different place. How long has it been since I've done that? I take my mug over to the sofa and sit with my legs up beneath me. I shouldn't have followed Matt like that, but it made me challenge myself for the first time in months. It made me try for a change. I sit up straight. This might be the craziest thing I've ever done. I'm talking about getting involved in someone else's life. This isn't right.

All at once, the nervous energy is back. I find myself on my feet and pacing around the living room. If I can focus on the Masons, surely I can focus on myself, too. If I can go to such lengths as to follow someone, I can do the same thing for *me*. I can improve myself; finally start to get better instead of hiding away in my house. Even as I'm thinking this, the doubts creep in. I shut my eyes and I'm in that pub, with the buggy eyes of the barmaid watching me. In frustration, I throw the glass at my fireplace, letting out a scream as the glass smashes.

That's not me. That temper is not mine. I never do things like that. No, I have to stop. It's time to turn my back on the Masons and forget about them once and for all. Matt Mason isn't the first knobhead to have an affair, and their marriage won't be the first to go tits up. It's time to focus on my own life. And the first step to that is shutting the curtains, going upstairs, and catching up on my work.

A weight lifts from my chest as I step towards the window. This is the right thing to do. But when my fingertips graze the satin of the curtains, movement from across the street catches my eye. It's April. She's standing there, right next to her window, dressed in bright red. I only see her to her waist, but the top half fits as though it's a sundress, with bows on the shoulder. She's wearing a light cardigan over the top. Something about her beautiful innocence forces a terrible sadness out of me. She will grow up to be a stunner, with that black hair and peachy skin.

I go cold all over. Only now do I see it. The teenager having lunch with Matt, she looked so much like April. Not in a way that would suggest the two were related, but in a way that makes me wonder about Matt, and whether he chose his mistress for a specific reason. I'm a little appalled at myself for thinking it. My fingers close around the curtains, and I'm about to shut them for good when there's more movement from April's room.

Suddenly her arms fly up and stay at chest height. I'm so taken aback by the sudden movement, that for a moment I concentrate only on the strange, drawn expression on her face. I don't notice the paper in her hands. She presses a white sheet of A4 paper up to the window, and then I understand what's happening.

The blood drains from my face when I see the message printed there. One word. Four letters.

HELP

I stagger back from the window with a hand covering my mouth. I knew that there was something not right about that family. I knew that something seemed wrong with Matt Mason. He's just... off. Someone who doesn't act the way you'd expect from a man his age. I saw him with that girl in the pub. Can you really trust a man having an affair with a girl that young? No, I don't believe that you can. April holding up this sign proves my suspicions. He's hurting her.

But what should I do?

April lifts the sign higher. Then she takes it away and wipes tears from her eyes. God, this is too much to bear. I have to help this girl. I start towards the door so I can go over there, but then I notice a figure walking down the street. I hurry back to the window to check. Yes, it's Matt. He's returning from lunch with his mistress. I direct my gaze back to April and then point to the street. April sees her father, snatches the sign away from the window and nods to me. Then she smiles.

I have to help her, but I need to think logically. If I go over there now, I can't take April away, and I can't physically stop Matt Mason from doing anything. He's much bigger than I am. But I can phone the police. I grab my phone from the sofa and dial 999. It's not the first time I've dialled 999. I've had to do it twice before. A shiver works up my spine, but I try to suppress the anxiety for April's sake. This is about her, not me.

"Emergency. Which service?"

"Hello, erm, I need the police. I think a little girl is in danger."

"What kind of danger? Can you give me the address?"

"Physical danger from her father. I think her father might be hurting her, but I... I don't know for sure. She put up this sign asking for help. The address is 72 Cavendish Street."

"Thank you. Now, can you talk through exactly what happened?"

"I'm sorry, there's not much more to say. The little girl seems very subdued and withdrawn in general. But today she put a sign in the window of her house saying help. I saw her screaming in the street a few days ago, too."

"Have you seen her father hurt the child?" the operator asks.

"No, nothing like that. Just what I told you."

"Okay, don't worry. We're going to send someone over to the house to find out what's going on."

"I don't want them to know I called. I'm their neighbour."

"I understand that, and we will not pass on your name.

But I do need to take your name, phone number and address so we can contact you."

I give the woman my details and hear typing on the other end of the phone. The hard and tight feeling in my chest is back. Matt must be inside now. The thought of him near that child makes my insides squirm.

"How long will they be?" I ask.

"Ten minutes. They're on their way now. You sit tight, Miss Abbott," she says.

I hang up the phone and stand by the window, keeping my body angled so that I'm out of sight. My mind is racing with all kinds of thoughts, such as Matt Mason finding out who called the police and breaking into my house in the night. Or the police pulling a raging Matt out of the house and him going crazy with a gun. *Don't be stupid, Hannah*, I tell myself. *This isn't America. No one has a gun here.* Not even the police, which I can't decide if I find it reassuring or worrying.

My thumbnail is bitten down to the skin by the time the police arrive. They didn't take much longer than ten minutes as the operator suggested. They pull up in a patrol car with the flashing lights. There are two of them, one woman, one man, and they are in their uniforms with big, clomping boots. They stride up to the front door and knock loudly. I can almost feel the vibration from the knock travelling across the street.

Matt opens the door. He's in the same clothes as before, but his feet are bare. His expression is pinched and worried when the police introduce themselves. In fact, his body language is defensive, with his arms folded and his back leaning away from them. I can't help it, I smile. *There you go,*

Matt. You can't get away with everything. Things do catch up with you. But the smile fades. *Things catch up with you.* The same can be said for my life.

The police go into the house and the door shuts. I'm left on the outside looking in.

LAURA

For once in my life I'm home at a reasonable time. I tried so hard to make sure all of my work was finished by five. I raced down all the back streets I could find to avoid the main traffic. But as soon as I set foot in the door, I felt a creeping sense of unease. Matt was being unusually nice, for one thing. He hasn't snapped at me once, and so far I've burnt the garlic bread that I insisted we had to have with the pasta salad, and I spilled red wine on the new sofa. But rather than fly off the handle, he's been more than reasonable. He's been understanding. That makes me think that something is going on, and I can't stop thinking about last night.

I caught a flicker of apprehension in his eyes when I found the receipt and accused him of cheating. It could be nothing, but then it could be more. My cheeks flush when I think of what came next, and then my stomach starts to hurt. I gulp down a little more wine.

"I'm plating up," Matt says.

We've pulled out the fold up table and perched it in the middle of the living room. April is already sitting on one of the chairs, and is scribbling in the little diary she keeps. Whenever I see her doing it, I get this irrational need to know what she's writing in there. Twice now I've lingered in her room, wondering if I could do it without her noticing. I found it under the bed once when I was hoovering. I was so tempted to open the cover, but I didn't want to be that kind of parent. I don't want to end up like *my* mother. An involuntary shiver passes over me just thinking about it.

"You cold, love? I can switch the thermostat up if you like," Matt offers.

The man likes it on 15 and won't have it any higher. He radiates heat like a walking hot water bottle. I do a double take when he offers to adjust it. "No, that's all right. I'm not actually cold. April, why don't you put your diary away now, chicken. Daddy is fetching tea."

April does as she's told, which I'm relieved about. There's a definite moodiness brewing, and God knows she's withdrawn and quiet, but at least she still does what she's told. I can't help but wonder how long that will last for. As soon as she hits the teenage years, things are bound to change. I'd better savour it while it lasts.

Matt sits opposite me, blocking the telly. For some reason we've left it on, even though none of us are watching it. The background noise is nice. It fills the silences.

"So what did you two get up to today?" I ask.

Matt glances at April. It's a quick, furtive look, almost like a warning. April pushes her food around her plate, scraping the porcelain in frantic motions. Her shoulders are hunched and tensed. Matt also appears on edge, but then he says,

"April was helping me with the car. I've been changing the fan belt..." he drifts into car speak that I don't really understand. I try to listen, I really do, but then my mind drifts off to thoughts of work. Matt knows straight away that I'm not listening, because his jaw clenches. This is usually where he rolls his eyes and lets out a long sigh, but not this time. "Sorry, honey. I'm boring you to death with all this car speak. How was work?"

I struggle through a particularly large bite of burnt garlic bread. I hadn't expected the conversation to come back to me so quickly. Matt usually talks about the car stuff for ages before getting to me. "It was good, thanks. They've decided to put the accountants on probation. The board is pleased with the decision and the company is moving forward. Crisis averted!" I laugh a little and Matt smiles along with me.

"That's great, babe." He reaches across and squeezes my arm.

My first instinct is to pull away, but I let him touch me. Matt notices my reaction, because a shadow of anger crosses his face, but then he breaks into another smile. One that doesn't reach his eyes. For a moment, we meet head on. We're both seeing each other, and we both know that our relationship isn't right. It's the kind of moment that creates a sudden urge to burst into tears. But I don't. I swallow them back down.

"Did you enjoy helping Dad with the car?" I ask April.

She looks up from her food and nods her head. I hadn't noticed before, but she hasn't touched most of her pasta. She's eaten the vegetables around the pasta, but only a third of her plate is cleared. And she's not touched the garlic bread at all. But then it is burnt, so I can understand that. I rack my brain, trying to think whether she's lost weight. Am I feeding her right? Am I failing as a mother for not noticing things? She's in a cute red dress with two bows on the straps, and a white cardigan. I remember buying the outfit. We were together in Marks and Spencer and for once both liked the same thing. It makes her come across as frighteningly mature and yet completely innocent at the same time. Looking at her, I'm overwhelmed by protective love. She's my little girl, the only child I have. That urge to burst into tears comes back again.

I wash the dishes, seeing as Matt made the tea. But I decide to pour myself a third glass of wine while I do it. As I plunge my hands into the hot water, I realise I'm a little light-headed. I can't handle my wine like I used to. Not like when I was twenty, anyway, but I am starting to develop more of a tolerance again. I suppose like all parents, I had a break from drinking a lot when April was younger. We were both so wrapped up in our family life that we didn't go out much. Matt especially. He started to believe that going out with friends was a waste of time, that we should be home with April, getting to know her and appreciating her growth into a person. But what I didn't realise, was that we were slowly isolating ourselves from our friends. As time went on, I lost touch with nearly all my old uni friends, and even a lot of Mum friends. Now I'm drinking again, but it's all at home. I'll open a bottle of wine at night and find myself finishing it before I go to bed. Matt disapproves. He says it's making me flabby.

I let the pots dry on the draining board, empty the sink, and quickly wipe down the surfaces. April is already back up in her room again. Matt isn't in the living room, which is where I thought he was, watching football on TV.

I make my way upstairs, seeing as I need the loo anyway—wine gives me a weak bladder—to hear low voices coming from April's room. It's odd for Matt to be in there at this time. Unless we need to talk to April, or need her to come downstairs, we tend to let her be, just popping our head in the door around nine to say goodnight before she goes to sleep. It's very rare that we sit and have a conversation with her. She hates us being in her room.

I move closer so I can hear a little better.

"... I think it's best we don't tell Mum about today, all right? You know what she's like."

April doesn't answer.

"You're a good girl, April. I know you'll do this for me."

I burst into the room. "Do what, Matt? What aren't you telling me? What is going on?"

April turns to Matt, with her eyes large and pleading. I notice then that they're quite red around the edges. She's been crying.

I sit down on the bed next to her. "What's happened? Have you been upset?"

"It's nothing," Matt says. "We're just feeling a little guilty."

"Guilty about what?" Alarm bells are ringing in my mind. I feel rigid with worry.

"April and I ordered pizza for lunch," Matt says. "April was feeling a bit sad about moving away from the old house, so we got it to cheer her up."

"Why would I be angry about you ordering pizza?" I ask.

Matt's story doesn't add up at all. There's something else going on.

"Because you came home early to eat with us and we weren't that hungry," he says with a laugh. "We've been trying to pretend all night, haven't we April? We just wanted it to be a special night, that's all. For once we're having family time, and we went and ruined it all by stuffing our faces at lunchtime."

"But I thought you didn't like pizza anymore, April?" I ask my daughter.

"I do." She nods.

Matt shrugs. "I thought so too, but I guess kids change their minds all the time."

Matt leans against April's chest of drawers as though he's completely relaxed. I can't put my finger on why I believe he's lying, but the truth is, I don't want to pry any further. I don't want to deal with Matt when he's angry, and if I press this any further I'll make him angry. The thought makes my stomach churn. I can't go through it, not tonight.

"So that's why you didn't eat your pasta, hmm?" I pull April closer to me and squeeze her shoulders. "If you're not happy, you know you can talk to me, don't you? About anything. I'm your mum, but I'm your friend, too." I cringe at the cheesy saying. Are parents ever friends? Is it even possible? I'm spinning a lie that has been told for generations. But we do it out of desperation, because the alternative—being kept at arms-length, never told anything—is too terrifying to contemplate.

"I liked our house," April says in a quiet voice.

It's small, but it feels like a breakthrough. She's talking to me about her feelings. That's big.

"That's because we lived there for a long time, and we have lots of great memories there. Don't worry, soon we'll have lots of great memories here, too. It just takes time. Are you worried about starting a new school?"

She nods.

"I moved when I was about your age." I find a spot on the duvet and concentrate on it, forcing myself to keep talking, but without thinking about that time in my life. I hate to think about it, but I want to help my daughter so I continue. "I was really scared. I thought I wouldn't make any friends at all. But on my very first day, I sat next to this girl in form time and she told me all about her summer, and the TV programmes she loved. We found out we liked the same music and films. We were best friends after just one conversation. It doesn't always happen like that, but it can. All you have to be is open to it. If you let people in, they'll be friends with you, and they'll like you."

I watch April, waiting for her to respond, but she doesn't say anything. I direct a questioning glance at Matt but he shrugs.

"Shall we leave you alone, kiddo?" Matt says.

April nods and offers me a small smile. It feels like a thank you, so I give her one more hug before getting off the bed. Matt and I leave at the same time, but I can't resist one last look at my daughter. She already has her diary out and is scribbling in it.

When I close the door to her room, I can't help worrying about how April *will* cope at school. The story I told her wasn't completely true. I did make a friend on the first day, Katie her name was, and we did end up being best friends for a long time. But I was bullied, too. I never had the right clothes, or the right hair and make-up. I was one of those poor kids that wear bargain knock-off trainers and smell funny. Katie was a natural martyr, someone who took pity on me.

I miss Katie a lot. We lost touch when she moved to London with her husband. At least, that's why I tell myself we lost touch. The truth is, when Katie first moved there, I went to visit them both a lot. Then Matt started going with me, and Katie stopped inviting us. Matt was going through a weird phase where he disliked all my friends. He'd get drunk at dinner and make an arse of himself, talking about how people who were politically left-leaning were all Communists. Katie works in charities and volunteers for the Labour party. It didn't go down well. Matt doesn't even *care* about politics. He just wanted to rile them up. I'll never forget the pitying expression on Katie's face when we last visited them. It was an "I'm so sorry you married him" look that I think about in my dark moments.

Matt has already settled into the sofa, and has the football highlights on, so I go into the kitchen and start putting away the dry dishes. I could try and convince myself that I'm not avoiding him, but of course it would be a lie. I don't want to fight, and I don't want anything else either. I just want to be alone.

I throw the empty wrapper from the garlic bread into the bin and notice that the kitchen bin is getting full. At first I open my mouth to shout for Matt. I hate taking the bin out. It stinks and can be heavy. But then I decide to do it myself. I quietly unlock the back door, pull the bin bag out, and nip into the garden to put it in the black bin outside. I have a sneaking feeling that what I see in the black bin will confirm my suspicions.

When I lift the bin, I see what I expect to see. There's one other bin bag in there, and it's a smallish one from the kitchen bin. There's nothing else. No pizza boxes.

I want it to stop. I want him to stop hurting us.

I thought it was going to be okay tonight. We had a nice dinner. We all got on okay for a change. Then Mum started asking questions and I had to lie. I thought she believed me, but later I heard her arguing with Dad again. I guess she started asking him questions and he got mad. They started shouting, then she ran upstairs and locked herself in the bathroom. I've put a chair under the door handle like Mum showed me to. I can hear Dad shouting and I'm afraid. I just want it all to stop. Maybe someone will help me.

HANNAH

Never have I felt like such a fool. The police thought
I was crazy. After they went into the Masons'
house, they'd left with big grins on their faces,
shaking Matt Mason's hand when they came out of the door.
I might have imagined it, but I'm sure one of them stared at
my window as they were getting back into the police car.
About ten minutes later, I heard a knock on my back door.
There, on the steps leading down to the garden, stood the two
officers.

"Hello, Miss Abbott isn't it? You made the 999 call about
the young girl across the street?" The male officer had spoken
first. He was only an inch or so taller than the female officer
and dwarfed by his uniform. He was young, mid-twenties,
and had blue eyes and blotchy skin. His voice had a hint of
Yorkshire accent, but wasn't as broad as most of the people
round here.

"Yes... I... it's supposed to be anonymous."

"We parked down the street," chipped in the female officer. She wasn't wearing her cap, so I could see that she was bleach-blonde. Her face was a little round, but pretty, and her eyes were brown which complemented her blonde hair. She was one of those girls who was a little bit chubby, but probably had a better BMI than most people. She was just shorter and stumpier. "I'm PC Ellis and this is my colleague PC Baker. Can we come in for five minutes? We just want a chat."

"I'd better... err..." The panic had started. My chest was tight and my stomach was churning. "Shut the kitchen door."

"That might be best," PC Ellis said.

It was only as I was stepping across the kitchen that I realised how much she sounded like she was talking to a child.

"Would you like a cup of tea?" I offered.

"That's okay." PC Ellis answered as she entered the house with the other officer.

My face flushed with embarrassment as they winced. I'd forgotten that it still smelled like sick from where I threw up. Then it flushed even more when both the officers saw the half empty bottle of vodka on the kitchen side. They'd exchanged a glance as though wordlessly speaking to each other. I didn't like the expressions on their faces. It was the kind of look that suggests they wouldn't be taking me seriously from now on.

"Must have left this out last night," I'd said, trying to force a chuckle into my voice. I'd put the vodka in the fridge and wiped the back of my hand across my forehead. Great, sweating would help convince them I wasn't drunk.

"Miss Abbott, we received your call at 12:30pm that a young girl had suggested she was in distress." PC Baker officer consulted his notebook. "We arrived at the scene at 12:43 and entered the property. We spoke to the girl, and the girl's father, but we saw no evidence of physical or emotional harm.

Now, what we'd like to establish, is why you decided to call 999."

The blood drained from my face. "Am I in trouble?"

"Not at all," PC Ellis said, although her expression suggested more "not yet". "We just want to establish the facts. We take child safety very seriously."

"Okay, well... for the last few weeks, since the Masons moved into number 72, I've heard shouting from the house. The parents seem to be fighting a lot."

"Have you ever seen anything physical?" PC Baker asked.

"No," I admitted. "But the shouting is very loud, and, I suppose I found it frightening." I hadn't told them that I'm frightened of my own shadow, that I worry if I sit down too long I'll get a blood clot and die, or that too much salt will give me a stroke.

He'd scribbled in his notebook and the silence stretched out unbearably. Even blondie shifted her weight from one foot to the other as though uncomfortable with the situation.

"Then, today, I was in my living room." My mouth went dry so I try to swallow, but ended up coughing instead. "I looked out of the window and saw the girl, April, standing at the window in her room. She just stood there for a moment, then she held up this sign." I'd mimicked holding up a sign.

"What was the sign like?" he asked.

"It was a plain piece of A4 paper. And on it she had written *help* in block capitals."

"What was the word written in?"

I frowned, wondering why that makes any difference. "Thick marker pen, or a felt tip or something like that. It was written large enough so I could see it from across the street."

"Uh-huh." The guy nodded. He finished scribbling in his

notebook and finally raised his head to meet my gaze. He flashed me a small, unenthusiastic smile. "And what can you tell us about your mental state when April held up the sign?"

"What does that have to do with it?" I snapped. Their friendly chat had started to become more of an interrogation.

"Please answer the question," PC Ellis had prompted. "It would be really useful for our investigation."

I swallowed again, my mouth completely dry. "I was... I was fine." It hadn't been convincing, not even to me.

"You hadn't been drinking?" she asked.

I closed my eyes and exhaled. "I had one shot of vodka." When I opened them again, I caught the end of an epic eye-roll from Baker. "It's not what you think. I'm not an alcoholic. I... I've been suffering with a little bit of anxiety for the last few months. I got worked up and drank the vodka to steady my nerves. But apart from that I was fine."

"So you didn't drink so much you made yourself ill?" Ellis asked, raising her eyebrows. I'd thought at least she was on my side. Not anymore.

"No, absolutely not."

"Okay, well thank you for your time."

They'd started heading towards the door and the panic of them being in my house made way for the panic of them leaving without making sure that April is safe.

"Wait, you're not going to leave April with her father are you? He's not a good guy. He's having an affair, and I think he might be violent," I said.

"It's not a crime to have an affair, unfortunately," Ellis replied. She'd fixed me with a pitying expression as she opened the door. "Miss Abbott, April is absolutely fine. She told us so herself. We're trained to search for signs of child abuse and we saw nothing. Look, she's a kid who was uprooted from a new home and she's probably just acting out. You did the right thing to call us if you were worried, but now it's time to move on... and maybe address your own problems."

Her words had been like a sting to my face. Even Baker seemed to feel sorry for me after what she said. And wasn't like she was being nasty, she appeared to be at least trying to give me some proper advice. As I'd closed the door, the embarrassment had enveloped me like a suffocating hug.

It took me a while to get over the visit from the police. I moped around the house for a while, unable to concentrate on my work, my mind completely swamped with differing thoughts about the Masons. When I see Edith going into the garden, I make a cup of tea and settle down on the step.

"Hello, love," she says, waving her sagging arm at me.

It's 5pm, but the sunshine is still unwavering, and the heat is still verging on unbearable. There's a very slight lingering scent of vomit coming from the doorway, but I reassure myself that it's all clean, and that I'm probably imagining it. A bee flies towards my face and I duck away quickly, spilling a little of my tea, but not before I notice a wry smile on Edith's face.

"You're a little jumpy today," she says.

"I didn't sleep all that well," I reply.

"You're too young to not be sleeping well," Edith says in a voice that's uncannily like the chastising voice of my late grandmother. She arranges her gardening tools on a little trestle table that her daughter's family brought over a few months ago. "Fresh air is what you need. When I was your age, I used to walk all over the place. We couldn't afford a car then, you see. They were a luxury, not like now when everyone has one. I used to walk to every shop. There was no going to the gym back then. Life was our gym."

And the world was her generation's dumping ground. That's why it's such a mess now.

"Edith, did you see anything strange at the Masons' today?" I ask.

"I've been out with my daughter today. She dropped me off an hour ago. The grandkids are growing up fast." She shakes her head. "Too fast. And all those blasted devices. They don't look up anymore. They'll be sorry when they're my age and have bad backs."

"Your grandkids are teenagers, aren't they?" I ask.

"That's right, thirteen and sixteen. Sam is taller than I am now. He's a strapping fella. Plays rugby, you know. Now there's a proper sport, not like those footballers kicking around a bag of wind."

I sip my tea and try to remain patient. I want to ask her a question, but staying on topic with Edith is like teaching a kid with ADHD. "What are kids like when they're a teenager, or almost a teenager, do they act up a lot?"

"Some do, I suppose," she says. She has her head down now, and she's re-potting a rose plant into a larger container. "It really depends on their upbringing. Parents need to take a stronger hand, stop all the messing about you see now-a-days."

"Do you think they crave attention?" I ask.

"Oh," she says with a laugh. "Of course! Don't you remember what it was like to be a teenager? You're younger than I am, so you have no excuse. Well, I had many brothers and sisters, and when they morphed into teenagers, well, they definitely wanted attention. They turned into complete pests, slamming doors, arguing with our parents, talking back. Don't give me that look, it's different than how the kids are today, we weren't rude in public, we respected our elders. But some of us did rebel against our parents, that's for sure."

"Were you a rebel, Edith?"

There's a sparkle in her eyes. "Now that would be telling." She lets out a sigh and straightens her back. She lifts her head up to the sky for a moment as though reliving a wondrous event. Then she's back to her rose plant. "Teenagers are a funny breed. It's frustrating to be so close to being an adult but so far away. I know I felt a sudden difference coming up to thirteen. It was like a big ball of frustration building up inside me. I wanted everyone to see me, but I wanted to hide away, too. Still, I wasn't as bad as my brother. When we got our first phone, he used to prank call everyone on the street! When Ma found out it was him, he got such a hiding. And my sister, well, she cut her hair right down, she did. Ma went crazy when she found out. Sally said it was because she saw the style in a magazine, but I know it was because she wanted to get back at Ma for stopping her allowance."

"I had no idea you knew so much about being young, Edith," I say with a smile.

"Well, when you get to my age, all you do is think about the past. All we ever want is to relive it. Well, some of it. I would not go back to being thirteen, that's for sure." Then she reconsiders. "Perhaps I would, I don't know. But, one thing I do know, it's a dangerous age."

"What do you mean?"

"It's trouble." She shudders. "Just trust me. I've had some run-ins with the bad-uns in my lifetime. There are some bad eggs out there. They want more than attention, trust me."

HANNAH

"I hope you like Sauvignon Blanc," Laura says as she steps into the living room.

It takes me a few seconds to stop standing there with my jaw hanging loose and actually close the door. When I'd heard the knock I'd considered leaving it. I don't think anyone has ever knocked on my door later than 5pm on a Saturday night, except for the occasional trick or treater on Halloween. I considered leaving it and shutting the blinds, but then curiosity won over panic, and I decided to see who it was. I never expected Laura.

"Yeah, it's great," I reply.

"Where's your corkscrew?"

"Umm, the kitchen. Second drawer down."

"I never get screw tops," she says. "I don't trust 'em."

I nod along as I follow her through to the kitchen. Laura seems so confident and at home even in my house. It's like she could exist anywhere and be the host. But why is she here? She must know, she must have guessed... A cold sensation prickles my skin. She knows I'm the person who called the police. She's come here to find out for definite. This is a test to see what I know.

I stand inside the kitchen door feeling like a stranger in my own home as she rifles through the kitchen drawer searching for the corkscrew.

"I know it's naughty, but I brought chocolate." Laura pulls a share size packet of Maltesers out of her bag and rattles it, grinning. "I'm supposed to be on a diet. I keep trying, but it's so hard." She pauses to set the bottle of wine on the counter, and I open my mouth to say she doesn't need to diet, but Laura begins talking again before I get the opportunity. "Matt's right though, I really do need to be healthier."

"Matt thinks you should diet?"

Laura plunges the corkscrew into the cork with such ferocity that it makes me start. "No, well, kind of." She sighs as she twists the screw into the cork. "He thinks I should exercise more. He says it quite a lot. He's a personal trainer, you know. Being healthy is really important to him. But it's not the be all and end all, you know? Oh, I'm rambling on already, aren't I? Going on about my problems and I've barely even said hello."

"That's okay." I force a smile. I can't stop analysing every one of Laura's moves. Does she know? Is her smile fake? Her movements are jerky and sharp. She keeps smiling, but there are times when her smile is frozen and unnatural. Is she anxious about something? I wish I knew her well enough to be able to tell.

Laura yanks the cork from the bottle and spins to face me. "Glasses?"

"Second cupboard to your right." I point towards the

correct cupboard, only to realise that my hands are shaking. As Laura turns away, I jam my hands in my jeans pockets.

"We can watch a film if you like," she says, picking up two wine glasses by the stem and letting them chink together. "Have you got Netflix? Or we could watch whatever talent show is on. Are you into reality stuff? I know you creatives can be a little pretentious." She winks as she shuts the cupboard.

"No pretentions here," I reply, aware of how small my voice sounds.

Laura pauses before she pours the wine. For a fraction of a second, her friendly expression fades and she appears sharper. For the first time, I realise that she has quite a pointed nose, and that her cheekbones are severe. Her hair is straight, without layers to soften it. Even her chin could be described as slightly pointed. She has a face that can never be completely open and friendly, there's always a hardness about it. My heart beats faster when her eyes are on me, scrutinising me. *She knows what I did.*

Then it's gone. She laughs. "How about The Voice, then? I'm a big fan so I'm a little relieved. Here." She passes me a huge glass of wine, filled almost to the brim.

"Thanks," I say, still feeling like a guest in my own home. There's an awkward little pause where the two of us stand there waiting for the other person to make the first move. Then I realise that this is actually *my* home, and I should be hosting. I move into the living room, making an odd gesture of "this way" with my hand.

"I'm glad we could finally do this," Laura says, settling into the sofa.

Rather than sit right next to Laura, I choose the armchair

on the other side of the room. I switch on the TV and put it onto BBC One.

"It's nice to get to know your neighbours, don't you think?" she says.

I nod. "Yeah it is."

"I mean, I don't really know anything about you, yet we live so close to each other," Laura says.

I shift in my seat and take a big gulp of the wine. I feel like everything she says brings us closer to what I did. What is she going to do? Attack me? Yell at me? I'm weak, I'll break down and admit it. I know I will. My back is sweating. This is going to be an awful evening.

"That's true," I say, avoiding Laura's gaze.

Laura sips her wine and the show begins. The silence between us is palpable, and I notice Laura's gaze roaming around the room. She's probably searching for clues about who I am, how I could call the police on her family. My face flushes. I gulp down more wine.

"Do you like living here?" Laura asks. "It's quite a quiet street, isn't it? Not much seems to happen."

"It is very quiet," I agree.

Laura drinks her wine. Almost half of it is gone already. "We didn't want to move. Well, I didn't want to move. It was mostly Matt's idea." Then she shakes her head. "That's a lie. It was my idea, but I didn't want to move *here*. It's too far out of the city. I have to drive for over an hour a day to get to work and back. The house is tiny. We could have got a bigger place closer to the city, but Matt didn't want to move to a bad neighbourhood. And he wanted a house that had been renovated so that everything is new. He's like that. He wants everything to look good."

"Oh," I say. "Sorry to hear that."

"It could be worse," she continues to watch the TV screen as she talks, in her own world. "We could be starving or homeless, I get that. But this whole transition is difficult. At least, it is when you don't want to be somewhere." Now she turns to me and laughs without humour, her hand flying to her mouth. "That's... that's not what I mean. I mean, I do *want* to be here, with my family. I wouldn't leave my family." But her voice is high-pitched, as though she isn't even sure if that's true. "I wish we hadn't had to move, truth be told. I was happy there. *We* were happy there."

I shift in my armchair, searching for the right thing to say. Laura doesn't come across as a woman seeking revenge on her busy-body neighbour. She seems to genuinely need someone to talk to. Maybe I got her all wrong. It wouldn't be the first time.

"You can be happy here, too," I say. The words feel strange. This conversation is alien to me. It's been so long since I talked about anything real. "I think sometimes it takes time to be happy when things have been rocky." I pause and sip my wine. "But you can be happy again." It's a lie. There are things that can change you so completely that happiness isn't an option anymore. That's just the way it is.

"Thank you," Laura says. She puts down her wine glass and tucks her feet underneath her. Her hunched shoulders relax, and the tension leaves her face. "What's your story?"

"Pardon?"

"Your story. Come on, I know you have one. You live alone. You don't have any photos on the walls or on the windowsills. You earn your living as an editor, so I know you must be smart and good at what you do. There has to be a reason why you live alone. Are you divorced?"

The wine isn't sitting right in my stomach. A hard knot begins to form in my chest. "No, I've never been married." Heat rushes up to my cheeks until I'm sure they're burning bright red. "There's no story, really. I used to go to University in the city. I lived with a boyfriend after uni but it didn't work out. Then I got my own place for a while. After I saved up, I came here." I told Edith the same thing when I first moved. It almost feels real.

Laura doesn't appear convinced, but she nods. "Well, maybe you'll find someone soon."

I appreciate the sentiment, but the words make me cringe. They aren't true, because once you've found the person you're supposed to be with, and you lose them, there's no second chance. That's it.

As we sip wine, the conversation moves on to my editing. I tell Laura a little about the kind of stories I edit and she even laughs at one of my jokes. I realise that I judged her wrongly. She didn't come here to torture me about phoning the police, she wanted someone to talk to. I start to wonder if she even knows about the police at all. Laura wasn't in when the police came. It was Matt who dealt with them. What if Matt didn't tell her? As the evening goes on, I feel more and more conflicted about the whole event. I should tell Laura about April's sign, but if I tell her, I also have to admit to calling the police. I could lie and say that someone else must have done it, but how convincing is that lie? The only other person who could see April's window clearly from their home is Edith, and she was out all day. It would only take one conversation for her to find out it was me. How could we live opposite each other knowing that I called the police on her family?

"I know Matt's trying his best," she says. "But he needs to do more. I'm the one paying the mortgage and shouldering the bills. Without his wages it's a real struggle, even after we downsized. Matt hasn't had a client for over a year now. I think it's time he got a job."

"Have you told him that?" I ask.

She shakes her head. "I daren't. He's so touchy these days." She rubs her palms along her jeans. She changes when she talks about Matt. Her posture changes. Right now she's crouched forward like she's moving into a ball.

"Are you and Matt... happy?" I ask. My heart beats faster and I drain the dregs from my wine glass. It's a bold question to ask, but I want to know. I *need* to know. If there's something not right between them, I have to tell her about April and the sign. I have to.

Laura starts with a smile and a nod. But her smile is stiff and awkward. "We're going through a bad patch. Matt's frustrated, I think. He hasn't got a lot to do, and I guess I rely on him too much with the housework and taking care of April. He's a house husband really. It's not good for him. I guess you've heard us fighting. I know we can be loud, sorry. Matt's been a bit touchy, but he's okay. He's getting better. More wine?"

I hold out my glass by the stem. Laura tops up the wine with a shaky hand.

"I'm sorry to hear about your rough patch."

Laura shrugs. "It's because money is tight. Once Matt finds a new client, everything will be much better."

I nod. "I'm sure it will be." I take a sip of my wine. I want to ask her more about Matt, but I don't want to frighten her away. Laura is far more closed up than she was when she first arrived. She wanted to talk, but I can see that she doesn't want to reveal too much. If I pry, I might go too far and then she won't tell me anything.

"How is April adjusting to the move?" I ask.

Laura lets out a long exhale. "I don't know. She's thirteen, it's a difficult age. I think she's attention seeking."

"The other day when she screamed... Has she done that before?" I ask.

"No, but there have been other strange behaviours. She writes in this journal all the time. I think she writes in it more than she talks to us. She's so quiet. She spends all of her time in her room. I just can't reach her, you know?" Laura sets down her wine glass and runs her hands through her hair.

As I'm trying to think of a way to respond, she pulls her phone out of her jeans pocket and stares at the screen. I have to tell her, and I have to do it now.

"I have to go," Laura says. She stands up and yanks her coat from the sofa. "Thanks for this, it's been fun, but Matt wants me home."

"Is everything all right?" I ask.

"Yes, it's fine." She shoves her feet back into her low-heeled pumps and opens the front door before I can do it for her. "I'm sorry I have to go. I'll come by another time. Or maybe we can go out for dinner?"

"Sure," I say.

Laura smiles at me as she leaves, but it's that same frozen smile she came with. I close the door after her, then watch her cross the street from the window. I never got an opportunity to tell her about April's sign. Laura disappears into her house, and we're left with the street between us once again.

LAURA

I had to get out of there. I was going to burst into tears just thinking about April, Matt and my life in general. I don't do that. I don't cry in front of strangers. That's for weak people, not for me. That's why I had to leave.

What a strange little house. It's like the house of a woman who never grew up. Nothing matches. The brown curtains and the faded wallpaper, the dirty carpet and the lingering smell of dirty laundry. If I lived alone in that place I would be depressed. Maybe Hannah *is* depressed, and that's why she never goes anywhere or makes any friends. Matt says he sees her at the window several times a day, not really doing anything, just watching. She's an odd woman, but I need someone I can talk to, and she's nice enough.

But I hadn't realised how I felt until now. I was so close to telling her everything. But I can't. If I tell her everything, she'll judge me.

Matt is in the garden with April when I get back. They're sat close together on the garden furniture. April has a can of Coke in her hand. She's nodding to whatever Matt is telling her. When they see me in the kitchen, Matt waves. He leans away from April and gives me a tight smile. It's the same expression he gets when he knows he's in the wrong.

What is he hiding from me? I thought Hannah might have revealed a titbit. If she really does watch us from the window, surely she would know if something was going on.

I wave back, and step onto the garden. It's no later than 7pm and the evening is a fine one. Our garden is one of the only enclosed gardens on the street. We have two fences that partition the space from the neighbours, but there's a gate for back access to some of the other houses. There's a shed at the bottom of the lawn, one of those outside lavatories converted after the loos moved inside. Matt was excited about the shed when we viewed the house. He said how he was going to paint it and put the washing machine inside to give us more space in the kitchen. I can't help wondering if he'll ever actually get round to it.

"You're back early," he says. He drags one of the fold out chairs next to his and pats the seat. "What's she like then? Is she as weird as she seems?"

I make a face. "She doesn't look weird." I settle into the uncomfortable chair, crossing and uncrossing my legs in an attempt to find a comfortable spot.

Matt snorts. "Come on. The girl looks like she hasn't been out in the sun for years. She's vampiric. And what are those clothes all about?"

"She's all right," I say, feeling defensive towards a person I thought the exact same thing about only minutes ago. But then I think of the concerned expression on her face as we were talking about Matt. She could be a warm person. Maybe at one point she was. Something has made her so isolated and alone, but I can't figure out what it was.

"Have you been drinking?" Matt says. "You stink of alcohol and your face is all red."

"We had a couple of glasses. What's the problem?"

"You know what the problem is." His voice is low, warning.

"For God's sake, Matt. It's Saturday night. I'm allowed a couple of glasses of wine."

Matt turns away. April rests her chin on her hand and lets her hair swing over her face so that I don't see her expression. I rack my brain trying to think up a topic of conversation that gets Matt away from my drinking, and hopefully gets my daughter to say more than two words to me.

"So what have I missed then? You two were thick as thieves when I came home. What were you talking about?"

April shrugs. "Just stuff."

"Well, what kind of stuff?" I snap.

"Stuff, Mum. Our game." She pulls up a knee and rests her cheek on it. I envy her then. When I was a teenager I could bend my body in ways I never could now. I could sprawl out on the floor without getting pains in my knees and back.

"Right. Well, sorry for asking. Sorry for wanting to know what my husband and daughter do when I'm not around." My face grows hot and tears burn at the back of my eyes. This isn't me. This snapping isn't me. I'm almost shocked at my tone of voice.

"You'd know if you were around more," April says. She gets to her feet and storms back into the house.

"Shit. I didn't mean to do that."

"You wouldn't have if you hadn't been drinking. How many did you have?" Matt grasps my arm with his large hand when I get up to follow April.

"That's none of your business," I reply. His hand squeezes my arm. I don't fight back, I sit down in the chair. He lets me go and I rub the sore spot where his fingers dug into my flesh.

"You know I don't like you drinking," Matt says.

I try not to look at him, but I can't help it. He's twisted away from me so I can't see his expression but I can see the tension in every part of his body. I get a fluttering of nerves in my stomach and I wish April was here with us. The idea that I don't want to be alone with my husband is suddenly very shocking. It's like a slap in the face with a bucket of cold water.

"You can't control me," I say with a shaky voice. "No matter how much you want to."

"*Control* you. *Control* you?" Matt gets to his feet, shoving the chair back so vigorously that I clench my fists in shock. "I have no control over anything, do I? Not you, not April, not even me. *You* pay the bills." He points at me, his finger jabbing towards my face. "*You* go to work every day. *You* provide, while I cook and clean like a fucking chump."

"You don't just do that," I say, using what I hope is a soothing voice. "You do more than that. You do more for *me*."

Matt pauses. "What's that supposed to mean."

I swallow, my mind racing. I need to make him feel like he matters. But that's hard when I'm struggling to remember why I fell in love with him at all. "I need you. You're here for me."

Matt scoffs and takes a step back. "That's a lie. A blatant lie. You couldn't give a rat's arse about me. Don't sit there and pretend that you rush home to be with me. With us. Don't do that. You're avoiding us. Admit it. Admit that you hate coming home to us."

I shake my head, tears brimming, swimming, drowning my eyeballs. I don't know what's worse, the realisation that he's right, or the fact that he's starting to frighten me again. "No. It's just that it's something I have to do. I have to work right now to make sure we have everything we need. We want April to have the best start in life, don't we? That's what we agreed."

"Well maybe I wouldn't have agreed to it if I'd known what it would entail."

"Don't say it—"

"Why not? It's true. We were fine before April came along. We shouldn't—"

Finally my anger breaks through the fear. I leap to my feet. "Don't ever say it. And don't you blame it all on me. It was a joint decision and you know it."

Matt sighs. "You're right. I know you are. I... I was wrong. I've been so wrong."

I step around him to leave but Matt grasps hold of my arm again. This time I do fight back. I wrench myself out of his grip. But Matt, with his mouth in a line, his eyes devoid of emotion, grabs the other one. There's a grapple, a tangling of arms and hands, and hands on arms. Matt's fingers press deep into my skin, forming bruises. I slap him around the face and he pushes me away. Before anything else happens, Matt turns his back, and I hurry back into the kitchen, hoping none of the neighbours saw our fight.

I rush upstairs, wiping my tears away. When I get to April's room, I stand there, trying to steady my breathing. I knock twice, and hear her voice: "Come in."

"Hey honey," I say. My voice is too bright. My smile feels fixed, even to me. My cheek muscles are aching. "I'm sorry about what I said. I shouldn't have snapped at you like that."

I push my way into the room, to find April standing in front of her bedroom window. Just like Matt, she doesn't look at me. April's room is not your typical teenager's room. There are no posters of One Direction on the wall. There are no teddy bears or framed pictures of besties. Her bedspread is a floral print I picked out from Debenhams. April didn't care what I ordered. Some of her stuff is still in boxes, as though she doesn't care about her belongings at all. I know most of her stuffed animals and old toys are in there. The rest of her things have been put neatly away. There aren't any clothes or glasses or crockery in her room. It's clean and it's tidy.

"Doesn't matter," April says.

I move towards her and put an arm around her shoulders. The act feels odd, like I shouldn't be doing it, like I'm encroaching on a stranger's personal space. April tenses up beneath my touch. I try to remember how I have to be patient with her.

"It does matter. I love you. You know that, don't you?" I say.

April's body quivers when I say the word love. "Yes."

I kiss her on the top of her head and let her go. "We'll spend some time together tomorrow, okay sweetie?"

"All right," she says.

I begin to leave, but then I change my mind and look at her one last time, staring out of the window towards

Hannah's house across the street. The sight of her standing there in silence—doing nothing but watching—makes me feel uneasy.

"You and Dad fighting again?" she asks, jolting me from my thoughts.

"No, honey. We're fine." I smile at her and back out of the room. For some reason, all I want is to get out of there.

But as I close the door shut, I could swear that I hear her whisper: "Liar."

HANNAH

I watch as the last drop of wine falls into my glass, creating ripples on the golden liquid surface. Since Laura left, I've been what my mother used to say: a bag of nerves.

Moving here was supposed to be calming after everything that happened before. I never wanted this dilemma to plague my mind in the way that it has. I never asked for this.

That woman left without knowing I'd called the police to her house because I suspected her husband of hurting her daughter. And now I have to decide whether to tell her every-thing—including the girl I saw Matt with in the pub—or telling her nothing. There's no middle ground here, either I break up a marriage on the slim chance that April is being hurt, or I potentially let a thirteen-year-old girl continue to be hurt. The police were so convinced that nothing was going on. So why am I still concerned? What could possibly make me believe April is in danger?

After sitting and finishing my wine, I yank my laptop

onto my knees and open Facebook. Maybe if I can get more evidence. Maybe if I find out more about Matt Mason... My heart starts thumping as I click "create an account" on the Facebook page. I can't quite believe I'm about to do this.

First, I have to find the right profile picture. That's where stock image websites come in. I've used them a few times when creating anonymous profiles for my editing services. I don't like people knowing what I look like, so I usually use a vector image of a smiling cartoon character. Anything that hides who I truly am. I can't remember who said it, but they remarked that everyone on the internet acts like they've had three glasses of wine. Well I'm on the internet and I have had three glasses of wine, so maybe I'm on my hypothetical sixth glass, and that's why I'm setting up a dummy Facebook account to befriend Matt Mason.

I find the perfect image of a smiling girl—probably about seventeen years old—with jet black straight hair and a cute button nose. I mentally apologise to the random model whose image I'm hiding behind, then upload the image to my new account. My name is Amy Manford. I am seventeen, I'm from Rotherham, and I'm studying sports science at college. I'm perfect. But I need something extra. My profile page is too thin, even after uploading a cover photo of a pretty land-scape somewhere in Yorkshire and writing a couple of statuses about enjoying hiking and the gym.

I need friends. No one is on Facebook without friends. But how am I going to do that when I'm a fake person? I have to make more sock puppet accounts.

It's a good job I have a subscription with the stock image accounts. Before I know it, Amy Manford has a number of friends and some distant family members from overseas. I have to be careful not to do too much. It has to seem realistic that Amy joined Facebook today, and her friends are posting messages on her wall saying how glad they are she finally joined.

When it's done, I reach out for my wine glass but it's drained. In desperate need of more courage, I hurry into the kitchen and pour a measure of vodka. Allowing myself to sober up and realise what an idiotic thing I'm doing would be a very bad thing.

No, it's not idiotic. It can't be. This is about Matt Mason. I'm almost one hundred per cent sure that he's not a good guy. I know it. He has a skeevy air about him, and about the way he lives. I can't get the image of him in the pub with that young girl out of my mind. Men shouldn't be allowed to get away with behaving like that. It's not right.

Amy Manford—my health conscious vibrant young woman—requests friendship from Matt Mason. Now, I wait for him.

I get up off the sofa to shut the living room curtains. April is standing at her bedroom window again. She's so frail and vulnerable. Am I the only one who sees it? Am I the only one who believes he could hurt her? I shake my head and snatch the curtains together. Then I pace around the room waiting for a Facebook notification. The vodka doesn't last long. Before I know it, I'm pouring another. The bottle is draining fast, but I won't be able to go to the co-op to buy another one tomorrow. I don't leave the house when I have a hangover. I can't.

I refresh the page. Matt Mason has accepted Amy's friend

request. I finish the last of my vodka and stare triumphantly at the computer screen. Now I've got him. Now I can get to the bottom of this once and for all.

A few seconds later, a red box with a one in it appears next to the message icon. I click on it eagerly, exhilarated and sweaty from the vodka.

Hey, hun. Do I know u?

I type back: *no, babe. Just liked ur profile pic.*
    Matt: *like what u c?*

My heart is beating so fast I'm terrified it might pop.

Me: *yeh. Ur hot.*
    Matt: *k, but tell me who u r. Did u really just find me?*

I don't know what's more disturbing, that Matt Mason is flirting with me as Amy Manford, or that he speaks like a fifteen-year-old on a chatroom, complete with text speak. It makes me wonder why Laura, an intelligent and together woman, would ever be with a man like him. They must've been young. I doubt that Laura is much older than thirty-five and April is thirteen. That would make sense.

. . .

Matt: *Well?*

    Me: *I just want 2 chat.*

    Matt: *k*

I settle into the sofa, and get to know the real Matt Mason.

Things are different now. I think it might be because of moving house, but Dad has changed. He used to tell me that he loved me more than anything in the world, and I should be grateful to have a father who loves me so much. I liked that. It made me feel special. But now I think he loves someone else more. Mum keeps asking him if he's having an affair. Then they fight some more.

I don't know if I want things to go back to the way they were. I was scared before, too. I guess sometimes I felt weird about everything. Sometimes I wonder if what happens in our house is normal or not. The only thing I do know, is that I don't want to listen to Mum and Dad fight anymore. Sometimes I hate them both so much. I hate Mum for never being around and always shouting at Dad until he yells. I hate Dad for what he does to her. And what he does to us.

LAURA

What the hell are these things? They resemble baby formula but smell rank. I pull out a large tub of Matt's protein supplement and remove the top. The powder drifts up to my nose and makes me sneeze. I wipe my nose, look around guiltily, and put the tub back in the cupboard. Matt changed when he started becoming obsessed with all this stuff. Before then he would never fly off the handle like he has been doing.

It's Sunday, and I had told myself that I'd take April to the shopping centre, but I woke up with a splitting headache and no desire to try to force April to have fun. Matt soon disappeared to the gym, leaving me with my teenage daughter. She wanted nothing to do with me. Instead she put her nose in a book, and went into the garden to sit in the sunshine.

I make my way upstairs with a duster and decide to quickly tidy April's room while she's out. I try to convince myself that I'm only here to dust and not to snoop, but deep down I know better. Matt's words cut me yesterday, when he said that April was a mistake. It was supposed to bring us closer together, but instead, she has driven a great big wedge between us. I run the cloth over April's chest of drawers. She used to have knick-knacks on all surfaces, little photo frames, ornaments of cats—she loved cats, always wanted one, but Matt won't have pets in the house—now there's nothing. There's only a lamp and her e-reader on her bedside table. Even the novelty alarm clock with the wagging tail hasn't made it out of the boxes.

I duck under the bed, checking there. I know she keeps her diary under her mattress, but I can't bear to open it. I won't be that kind of mother. Not like mine. She snooped on everything I did. Both my parents were complete control freaks. They had to know everything all the time. Maybe that's why I ended up with Matt. I shut that thought down. If I go there, I'll let those feelings in, and I don't want to do that.

My fingers find a piece of paper under the bed. I pull it out and am about to screw it up when I notice the word scrawled across the page. I'm standing there, completely transfixed by this one word, trying to think what it could mean. Then I turn around and I gaze out of the window towards Hannah's house, remembering the way April was staring out of the window yesterday. Could this be a sign? It can't be. Can it? She wouldn't.

I hurry out of the door and down the stairs, taking them so fast I almost collide with the front door on my way down. I must've burst through the back door into the garden because April lifts her head from her book and appears completely gobsmacked. Her jaw hangs open as I stride across the grass. In fact, it's the first real expression I've seen on her face for months.

"What is this?" I hold up the sign.

April's face drains of blood. Her already pale skin fades to ivory in the summer sun.

"What have you done?" I insist. "Tell me." The fact that she's still holding that book infuriates me all the more. I yank it from her hands and toss it onto the floor. "Please tell me that you haven't been holding signs that say help against the window. Tell me you haven't."

She doesn't say a word. I watch as she looks away, finding some spot out in the distance to stare at.

"Why would you do this to us, April? Don't we take care of you?"

Then she meets my gaze and her eyes flash with anger. Her upper lip curls up as if in a snarl, but then the expression breaks, and tears flood her eyes. She's back to being a young girl again. I take a step back, surprised by her reaction. She was genuinely angry with me. What am I missing? What has caused her to be like this?

"Everything all right?" Matt saunters into the garden with his gym bag slung over his shoulder. "What's going on?"

I hold up the sign. "April has been holding this sign up in her bedroom window."

"Oh," Matt says.

I stare at him, aghast. "Oh?" I see the warning in his eyes. I see the lack of surprise in his expression. "You knew about this, didn't you? That's what you've been keeping from me. I *knew* something was going on. What the *fuck*, Matt? You don't keep something like this from me."

"Don't overreact," he says. "It was just a prank. April and I sorted it all out. There's nothing to worry about."

"Nothing to worry about, are you kidding me? Our teenage daughter holds a sign up in the window asking for help and you think there's nothing to worry about?" I chuck the paper to the ground and put my head in both of my hands, completely at a loss as to why all this is happening. After a few deep breaths, I say, "April, why did you do this?"

She shrugs and sniffs away a few tears.

"Laura, you're overreacting to this. She's acting out, that's all."

"Was it a prank?" I say to my daughter, ignoring my husband.

April turns to Matt before she answers. "Yes." Why is she always seeking out his approval before she answers every question?

Now I don't know what to think. Do I really believe that April wants help from a stranger? Not really, no. But there seems to be more going on than what April and Matt are letting on.

"Tell me. Tell me now why you did this." I put both hands on April's shoulders. She angles her head down and I see a tear drip from the end of her nose. "No more crocodile tears. Tell me why you're doing this."

"Stop pushing her," Matt says. "She won't talk to you like this."

"Would you just *shut up*," I snap. "Stop undermining me."

Matt laughs without humour. "That's fucking rich coming from you."

April wriggles out of my grip and goes back into the house.

"Hey, don't you walk away from me when I'm talking to you." I snatch up the sign and follow her into the kitchen.

"Stop yelling at me," April whines.

"I'll stop yelling when you tell me why you would do this." My hands are shaking when I point at her. Even in the heat of the moment I'm beginning to wonder why I'm acting like this, why I'm flying into such a rage. Matt and I can go at it when we're mad at each other, but I've never been like this with April before. But for some reason I can't calm down, and I keep blurting out whatever comes into my head.

April pours herself a glass of water and hovers next to the breakfast bar. The fact that she paused to do that mid-fight is ridiculous. Before I even know what I'm doing, I've closed the space between us, snatched the glass out of her hands, and thrown it at the wall. April screams and dives through the open kitchen door into the living room.

"You're insane," she screams. "This is why I want help. To get away from your insanity. From both of you!"

"What are you saying, April?" Matt says in a low, menacing voice. "Maybe you should be careful about what you say that you can't take back."

April's chest rises and falls quickly as she backs away from us. I'm crying, she's crying. Matt drags his hands through his hair. Everything is a mess.

"April, I'm sorry," I say. The silence that comes next hangs in the air like low fog. No one moves. Then April runs up the stairs away from us, her footsteps soft on every step.

Matt's hand is on my arm and he twists me around to face him. His hand is up and the next thing I know, I'm reeling from two short, sharp slaps around my face. "What did you think you were doing? Why did you react like that? Look what you've done to our daughter. Fuck! That busybody across the street was right to call the fucking police."

"What did you just say?" I stroke my sore cheek. "Did you say the police?"

Matt pushes his hands into his pockets and hangs his head. His nose whistles as he exhales. He's been caught out and he knows it. "The police came round and asked some questions."

"*What?*" I can't believe the amount of lies that are between us all. I was wrong about being able to fix my broken family. This is too much. It's all too much of a mess. "The *police* were here about our daughter and you didn't tell me?"

"I'm sorry, all right. I didn't want to worry you."

I half-collapse onto the sofa. "I can't believe this."

"I can't believe her." Matt's voice comes out in such a low growl that my head snaps up. I follow his gaze out of the window. On the other side of the street, with her hand pressed up against her living room window, Hannah stands, staring at us.

HANNAH

It was the sound of the glass smashing that caught my attention. I pulled myself off the floor to go to the living room window. All of the Masons were there, and they seemed angry. April screamed before running upstairs, then Matt slapped Laura across the face. I stood there, completely frozen, completely transfixed by what I was seeing, like a person watching a soap opera. Then they both turned to me, and I have never seen hatred in anyone's eyes like I did in Matt Mason's. I rushed straight to the phone and called the police.

After making my Facebook profiles, Matt continued to flirt with me for a while longer, but he didn't do anything that could be construed as cheating. Things didn't get sexual, but it was still very inappropriate coming from a man his age directed at a girl Amy Manford's age. If she was real, of course. But I ended up finishing the bottle of vodka and falling asleep on the living room floor. At about 4am I awoke startled from a nightmare, the same nightmare I have almost every night. But this time it was different. This time I saw

April's face in my dream, and I think even then I knew something bad was going to happen today.

Now I'm pacing the living room, wearing a track into the carpet. My hangover is contributing to the rising nausea. I'm waiting.

I didn't call 999 this time, I called PC Baker, who left me his card on his way out the door. But now I regret that decision. I thought he might react faster, and I thought I came across saner, but now I wonder if he had already decided I was a whackjob and decided not to take me seriously. Why did I drink last night? Why did I befriend Matt like that?

I try calling Laura's mobile to see if she and April are okay, but after five attempts and two texts, there's nothing. The curtains are shut across the street, so I can't see anything. I go through to the kitchen to make a drink, just water this time. I stand by the kitchen sink waiting for the tap to stop spluttering. Then I lift my head and drop the glass when I see what's in the garden. It smashes all over the kitchen tiles.

The glass is on me.

I ignore it. Instead I grab my keys and hurry out into the garden. There she is. April. There she is before me.

"April," I say. My voice is breathy and rushed. "Are you all right? What are you doing here?"

The girl has been crying. There are tear tracks down her cheeks, and red rings around her eyes. Her chin quivers as she moves away from me.

"April, talk to me."

Slowly, she unfolds her arms from around her chest, and pulls up the sleeve of her shirt. I hear the sharp intake of my breath before I'm aware of making it. Along April's upper arm is a series of deep blue bruises.

"Who did this?" I say, in that same breathless voice.

But she won't answer me. She won't speak at all. Another tear falls from her nose. She turns her head away.

"Come into the house. I'll make you a cup of tea and we can talk about this. You're going to be all right, April. I promise. If you tell me everything, I'll make sure you're all right." I realise now that *I'm* going to cry. The nausea has gone, but it has been replaced by a burning desire to burst into tears. I feel so... so... protective of this birdlike, vulnerable girl standing before me in my garden. I want to take her in and look after her. I want to beat Matt Mason black and blue for doing this to her.

I reach out to touch her, to brush away one of her tears. But she jerks back. In mere moments she's running away. Her hair stretches out behind her, black and glossy like a raven's wing.

"April," I call, starting to run after her.

But she's gone.

I rub my face with my hands, feeling numb and helpless. This can't be it. This can't be where I fail to save her. I have to do more. I rush back to the kitchen, pick up my mobile phone from the dining table, and punch in the number from the business card left to me by PC Baker.

"Hello, is this PC Baker?" I ask when the phone is answered.

"Speaking."

"It's Hannah Abbott," I say. I might be imagining things, but I could swear that I hear a sigh down the other end of the line. "Listen, I know I've rung you once already, but this is really important. April Mason has a series of bruises on her upper arm. The left one."

"How the bloody hell do you know that?" PC Baker sounds almost suspicious.

"What? Well, I know because she showed me. She turned up in my garden and showed me her arm. I... I didn't ask to see. She just showed me."

The man sighs again. "All right. I'll be over there in less than ten minutes. Okay?"

LAURA

The bang on the door is ominous. Neither I nor Matt move. He's still staring at the closed curtains. I hesitate before going to the door. April came downstairs but I couldn't look at her. She said she was going to make a snack and disappeared into the kitchen for a while. A few minutes ago she went back upstairs. None of us spoke as she went up the stairs.

"If it's that cow from across the street tell her to fuck off," Matt says.

"Don't worry, I will," I reply.

I can't believe Hannah. She let me sit there and talk about my problems while all the time she knew what April did, and she even called the police. She thought my daughter was in danger and she didn't even tell me. What kind of a person does that? Then, to top it all off, she's tried to ring me at least five times today. I have no idea what kind of narcissist thinks they can do that to another human being and then call for a chat.

When I swing open the front door, my jaw almost hits the

floor. Before the two police officers can speak, I hear myself saying. "The bitch called you again. I can't believe it."

The man frowns, before examining me from top to bottom. "We had a call about a domestic disturbance. Can we come in please?"

I step back from the door, allowing them to pass. The police officers are immediately roaming around the room, staring at everything—the walls, the carpet, the furniture. I know already that they're searching for signs of a struggle. They're checking to see if we've been physically fighting. The thought of them analysing our actions makes me feel sick.

"How can I help you?" I ask. I realise that I look a mess. I glance quickly in the mirror and smooth my hair. There isn't a bruise from where Matt slapped me. That's one good thing.

"I'm PC Ellis and this is my colleague PC Baker. Can we speak to your daughter April for a moment," says the younger, female officer. She has one of those "approachable smiles" like a receptionist, or the girl who tries to nick your boyfriend from under your nose. I dislike her immediately.

"Why?" I ask. I fold my arms across my chest and stand between them and the stairs.

"The call was about your daughter, Mrs. Mason. We're just following up. It won't take a minute." She speaks with a soft voice like she's talking to a child and I hate it.

I open my mouth to tell her where to go, but Matt must sense that I'm about to do something stupid, because he gets to his feet and stops me. "I'll go and get her." Then he says to me, "The sooner this is over and done with, the better."

PC Ellis continues to smile at me as Matt disappears up the stairs. I can see the sickly sympathy emanating from her patronising expression. I think she believes I'm some battered wife to be pitied. But she knows nothing about me and nothing about my family.

I rake my fingers through my hair. Who am I kidding? My family is in tatters.

"Are you all right?" she asks, coming closer to me. "Would you like to sit down and have a glass of water?"

I shake my head. I want to turn time back. I want to go back a long way.

Finally, April and Matt come back into the room. I shift my weight from one foot to the other. What has that crazy bitch said across the street?

"Look, all right, we did have an argument," I say before the questions begin. "I found out that you guys had been here before because April held a ridiculous sign up to the window. I was angry at April for what she did, but I didn't hurt her. No one has hurt her. She's acting out because we just moved here. That's all it is. She's a troubled child in general, but no one is hurting her. This is a safe home." Matt places a hand on my arm and I stop speaking. I'd been rambling at a fast pace, but I didn't realise it. I must seem like a hysterical, stupid woman to them.

"April, do you remember me from a few days ago?" she asks in a voice more suited to talking to a toddler than a teenager.

April nods.

"You're not in any trouble, okay? We just want to establish what has been happening here. We want to hear from you how you are. You can talk to us, okay?"

"I'm fine," April says. "I'm sorry about the sign."

"She is, she really is," I add. Matt glares at me.

"That's good. We don't mind about the sign, we just want

to find out a bit more about you. Is there anything you'd like to tell us?"

"She just said she was fine," I reply through gritted teeth.

"Can we see your arm?" the woman asks.

What is this about her arm? My face flushes hot with embarrassment and fear. Why am I the last to know everything? Matt's expression is impassive. If this is new to him, he doesn't show it.

April rolls up her sleeve and my heart drops when I see the bruises. There are at least two of them, and they're very dark blue. I try to control my breathing, pretending that I'm not shocked to see the deep bruises on my daughter's arm. But inside I'm crying. I've failed at being a mother.

"How did you get those bruises, April?" the woman asks.

"I fell down the steps into the garden," April says. She doesn't miss a beat with her answer. I could breathe a sigh of relief, but I can't seem surprised, not now.

"I saw the whole thing," I say. "It was a real tumble. We didn't have any steep steps at our last place. She's lucky she didn't bang her head. It's not as bad as it looks, I promise. There's no damage to the bone or the joint."

"Are you in the medical profession?" PC Baker asks this time.

"No, but I made sure April could move her arm after the fall. And I checked in with NHS Direct."

The officers assess me for a moment, narrowing their eyes. Then PC Ellis smiles, apparently satisfied with my explanation.

"Look, this is all a huge mistake," Matt says. "The woman across the street has some sort of obsession with us. She clearly has no life of her own, so she's trying to ruin ours.

She's called Laura five times today, and sent her text messages. Show them your phone, love."

I pull my phone out of my trouser pocket and scroll down to the missed calls section. Hannah's number features many times. The male officer jots down the number into his notepad.

"She's called the police on us twice now, and both times it's been over nothing. No one else has a problem with us on the street. They don't think we're hurting April, it's just her. You've no idea how hard it is to have someone accuse you of something so awful. She's making our life hell. That's why we keep arguing, because of her. It's Hannah you need to talk to, not us. She's a compulsive liar. She's a writer, you know. She understands how to make up stories. I bet she gets them all confused in her head, everything gets embellished." Matt is so impassioned that even I find myself siding with him.

"If anyone was hurting April, I would know," I say. "She's my little girl and I would do anything to protect her."

The two police offers exchange a glance.

"We'll look into this for you," PC Baker says with his mouth in a tight line.

HANNAH

When the police come out of number 72, I know it's all gone horribly wrong. I expected Matt Mason in handcuffs, but they leave alone. It's Laura who shows them out. She watches them leave from the door, but as they're getting into the patrol car, her gaze redirects to me. I've never seen anyone so angry before. Her narrowed eyes dagger me. I shrink back away from the window, my stomach like a washing machine.

What am I going to do?

The buzz from last night is wearing off, leaving me to contend with a dank, anxious reality. Even my house smells dirty; musty and mouldy, like the sweat leaving my body. I'm unwashed and greasy, wearing yesterday's clothes, pacing the room like a tethered animal. They let him go. Now April has to live there with that monster. That cheating, lying, skeevy man.

I gasp when the phone rings, wrenching me from the dark fog of my mind. I leap back and my heart thuds. I cross the room and grab the receiver.

"Hello?" I say, my voice almost unsure of itself.

"Hannah Abbott? This is PC Baker. We're calling to ask you to come to the police station tomorrow morning. We'd like to talk to you about your allegations against Matthew and Laura Mason—"

"Not Laura," I say. "Just Matt. He's hurting April, you have to believe me."

The officer sighs. "Miss Abbott, you must not contact the Masons anymore. We'll talk to you in more depth tomorrow about this, but from now until then, you must not contact the Masons at all. Do you understand?"

"Are you going to arrest Matt? Did you see the bruises on April's arm?"

"Yes, we saw the bruises," he says, avoiding my first question.

"And you're not going to do anything about it?"

"That's not something I can discuss with you over the phone." His tone is firm, to the point of patronising. "I need you to confirm that you will not contact the Masons. This is very important. I need to ensure that you were listening to me."

I'm taken aback. Not only have the police done nothing, they've called me and practically warned me from speaking to the Masons. They're painting *me* as the villain.

"Miss Abbott," He repeats.

"I will not contact them," I say. I slam the phone down so hard I hope it made his ears ring.

This is unbelievable. Not only has Matt Mason got away with what he's done to that little girl, but his wife—and even the police—are supporting him. I reach for my phone to try Laura's number again, maybe if I can reach her I can explain everything that has been happening. I could kick myself for not telling her when I had the chance. Now she doesn't trust me. I put the phone down before dialling, thinking about the conversation with the police. Contacting the Masons wouldn't solve anything.

The dark fog of my anxiety swirls up from my toes. Every part of my body is tightly wound. I need something to help me calm down. *Get through the next ten seconds.* No, fuck off, I won't. I'm not playing that game anymore. I stagger into the kitchen and pull bottles out of my kitchen cupboards. There has to be alcohol in here. The vodka is gone, but there must be an extra bottle I've forgotten about. Aha! I grasp my new saviour, an old bottle of whiskey given to me at one long ago Christmas. A ghost of my past.

Whiskey is not my first choice of spirit. I almost spit it out when I take a swig, but then I swallow it down and the heat spreads through me, working out the knots that have tightened my chest for too long. This is the beginning of a new determination to stop the panic taking over my life. I refuse to be that timid woman afraid of the world. I will go out there and grasp it, with the help of my new friend—whiskey.

There's the sound of movement outside. I twist towards my kitchen window to see Edith in the garden staring open mouthed at the bottle of whiskey in my hand. I take another swig, maintaining eye contact, then I flip her the middle finger. Judgemental old bat. She has no idea what I've been going through. She has no idea who I am. I'm just the woman with nothing to her. I'm a mild inconvenience, with a car I won't sell and a garden I won't tend. A woman with no husband, no life, no child—that is not someone she can respect. To her generation my worth comes from how many kids I can pop out.

I think of every judgemental look I've had when people realise my age and see no ring on my finger or child holding my hand. I take another swig. If only they knew the first thing about me.

But now I have the chance to save a child, and what am I going to do about it? Am I going to sit back and let it happen?

I haven't eaten for hours, and I've had virtually no sleep, but I don't think about any of that when I approach my front door. I don't think about my mental state as I open the door, leaving my whiskey on the door step. I'm not thinking as I cross the road and pound on the Masons' front door. But I do see April upstairs watching me. She waves once and I nod to her. Someone has to look out for her.

Laura opens the door. She keeps the chain on so half her body is visible. For once she isn't as pristine as usual. In fact, she's almost haggard. There are bags beneath her eyes, and her hair is unruly, poking out from a messy ponytail. "You're not welcome here. Come any closer and we'll call the police."

"What does your husband do when you're at work, Laura?" I say. "Where does he go? What does he do to April? Why is her arm bruised?"

"How do you know about the bruises on her arm?" Laura asks through her gritted teeth.

"She showed me," I say. "She came to me and showed me because she needs *help*."

Laura shakes her head. "You're crazy."

"Well, your husband is having an affair, did you know that?" I say.

Laura's face pales. "What are you talking about?"

Now I know I've got her attention. Talk about her daughter and she doesn't give a shit, but her husband having affair she cares about. "I saw him in the pub with a girl. And, do you know what? She can't have been more than nineteen. She had dark hair and pale skin, just like your daughter. Your husband is sick."

I stagger back when Matt appears at the door. He unhooks the door chain and is out on the front step in an instant. I feel the eyes of the street behind me, watching the spectacle.

"What are you accusing me of?" His eyes are wild. I'd forgotten how intimidatingly huge he was until he loomed over me making me feel like running away screaming.

"I saw you with that girl. Then I came home, and April put a sign in her window asking me for help."

"I don't know what you thought you saw, but it's a lie. You're drunk, and you're pathetic. Get the hell away from us and stay away." He comes so close to me that I long to shrink away. But instead I hold my ground.

"No," I say, with tears in my eyes. "I'm not a drunk. I saw you. And I want to help your child. I want to keep her away from *you*."

Matt takes a step forward. "Get away from us."

"I will not." I straighten my back. "You're a liar and a cheat. I saw you slap your wife. What else have you done to them both? There's more. That's right, I know more about you than you realise." I can't help it, I grin. "I'm Amy Manford."

"Who the fuck is Amy Manford?" he says.

"The seventeen-year-old girl you befriended on Facebook," I say. "That was me. I pretended to be her."

"You're mad," he says. "You're actually insane." Matt shakes his head and pulls his fingers through his hair.

It's then that something snaps inside me. It's the thought that he can go back to his life as though nothing has happened while I'm left alone with nothing. He doesn't deserve a family. I would give anything, anything... and he hurts the family he has.

It all happens so fast that I barely know what's happening. I'm on his back, kicking and punching anything I can reach. Then Laura is flying at us both, her caramel hair flying in the wind. She screams at me, trying to pull me away. One of the doors opens from down the street and a man runs at me. He grabs me beneath the arm pits and drags me away, but I'm struggling against him. I break free and run at Matt again, knocking us both onto the tarmac. His hands are up, protecting his face. Two men lift me off him. And then the police sirens wail.

HANNAH

There's the crunch of metal and a spray of glass flies through the air. My face is punched by something pressurised before the glass lands over me. I'm dazed, but I know something is badly wrong. When I see the blood I start to scream, and I don't stop.

My back is sore and stiff when I wake up in the police cell. It really is as uncomfortable as it looks on the television. The panic that seizes my chest is almost overwhelming. This isn't my bedroom. This isn't my house, my one safe place in this world of danger. I throw up in the tiny sink, before crawling back to the cot, pulling myself into the foetal position.

A police officer comes by to give me a glass of water, which I gulp down before throwing up. My head hurts almost as much as my chest and back. I lean forward and sob into my hands, remembering everything that happened the day before.

"You know, you can really sleep." The door opens and PC Baker walks into the cell. "I've been waiting all night to question you."

"Why didn't you wake me?" I ask.

"Figured I'd let you sleep it off. Come on. Time to have a chat," he says.

I hold out my hands for the handcuffs but he just smiles. "No need for that. Just follow me. Have you eaten yet?"

I shake my head.

"Want to eat?"

I shake my head again.

"We'll get you some more water. This way." He leads me down the corridor and into a sparse interrogation room.

My eyes trail the grey walls, trying to find the two way mirror, or camera, or whatever else is there to record me.

"You were arrested for assault yesterday, Hannah. Do you remember that?" he says. He nods to PC Ellis as she steps into the room. I can't shake the feeling that when they're dealing with me, they both talk to me as though I'm a child.

They think I'm mentally ill. The realisation is like a slap to the face. They don't just believe I'm a busy body or an idiot, they actually think there's something wrong with me. And, really, are they incorrect? Can I really dispute the facts?

"Yes, I remember." I stare down at my hands. They both tremble, partly from the panic still holding tightly onto my chest, partly from the hangover. *Breathe, Hannah.*

"Hannah, can you tell us why you've been harassing the Mason family since they moved into Cavendish Street? They don't seem to have done anything to you, and yet you've reported them to the police twice, you've created multiple Facebook accounts to stalk Matt Mason, and you've been repeatedly calling Laura Mason."

"You shouldn't ask me, you should ask their daughter. He's hitting her, and... and maybe more, I don't know. I saw him in a pub with a student girl who looks like April. He has a type, you see—"

"Hannah, the girl you saw Matt Mason with in the pub is a student, yes, but she's his personal trainer client."

"No, I say. Students can't afford that."

"This one can," the detective says. "She's from a wealthy background and very health conscious. There's no law breaking going on there."

My heart drops. What if I've been wrong?

"April Mason admitted to holding the sign to the window. She said it was a prank. I'm afraid the girl is quite troubled, but we don't believe there is any abuse going on. Nothing has been reported from medical professionals. Neither Laura or Matt have any previous convictions. We're going to keep an eye on them from now on, but there's no reason to arrest Matt Mason," PC Ellis says. She leans forward and her voice changes. We're back to *that* tone. The careful tone used for vulnerable and unpredictable people. "Now, Hannah, I understand that seeing the sign from that young girl must have been quite distressing. We've looked into your past—"

"No," I whisper.

"Yes," she says. "And I'm afraid that your behaviour makes a lot more sense after finding out what happened a few years ago. I'm talking about the accident."

"Please don't." There's no air in here. I can't breathe.

"We know you had a breakdown after the accident. We know that you spent some time in a psychiatric unit. Have you been taking your pills, Hannah?"

I can't speak. I can only shake my head.

"It must have been very difficult seeing April Mason in distress after losing your own child like that."

"Stop it." I put my head in my hands. The air is thick, it's like breathing in mud.

I want her to stop talking, because every word takes me back there.

Get through the next ten seconds.

The glass. The crunch of metal.

"Community service, a driving ban, and a fine. It doesn't seem like much for what you did."

I shake my head. My mouth opens to speak but the only sound that comes out is a desperate gasp. I move my hands down to my throat, where the air is stuck, like a hard lump. My vision starts to blur as the dizziness takes me over. I long for home where it's safe, where I know I can avoid the memories.

I scream when I see the blood and I never stop screaming.

She's right. It was all my fault. I was arguing with Stu again. This time it wasn't about what he did, it was about being late. I was supposed to be ready when he got home, but I wasn't. We had to rush. He didn't want to drive. It was his big night and he deserved a drink. I agreed to it this one time, because it was a special night. He was supposed to collect an award for bravery. He was a fireman, and he'd saved a family from a terrible fire. We'd decided to take our three- year-old with us...

Cold seeps over my skin. I don't see the police officers, or the interrogation room. I see the broken glass and the blood.

"Ms Abbott, are you all right?"

Then the floor is coming up to meet me.

"Someone get a paramedic in here. Call an ambulance."

"**F**uck's sake, Hannah. How long are you going to be? I got changed at work so I wouldn't be late. You were supposed to pick me up with Emma."

"How many more times. I'm sorry," I shout from downstairs while scurrying across the bedroom with a pair of high heels in my hands. I can hear Emma start to cry followed by Stuart comforting her. If he knew what a nightmare it had been this afternoon. He doesn't understand how hard Emma can be. He doesn't understand how much attention she needs because he's never here. He's either at work or...

A hard lump forms in my throat. I can't think about *her* tonight. I won't let her spoil it. Stu had a blip, but he came back to me and that's what matters. I might still be carrying baby weight, have wrinkles around my eyes, and constantly smell like a sticky toddler, but I am his wife. The woman he said he would love for the rest of his life. She was some cocky young rookie at the fire department. She was a petite piece of temptation that he fell for at his weakest point. I always knew that he had a hard job, and that's why I made allowances for him. I allowed him to play football rather than babysit Emma at the weekends. I allowed him the nights out and the hangovers. But this was too much. It almost ruined everything.

"Hannah!"

The urgency in his voice hurries me up. I almost trip coming down the stairs. In the hallway I jam the shoes on my feet, glance once more in the mirror, and grab my clutch bag.

"All right, I'm ready. Let's go."

"Mummy pretty."

"Thank you, darling." I crouch down next to my daughter and pull her into a tight hug. The smell of her, the warmth of her, eases the tension in my body. I let out a laugh that's almost a sob. Even after three years she surprises me with how generous and loving she is. I pull back, and brush her hair away from her face. She's almost all Stuart in features, but me in colouring, with my brown eyes and brown hair.

"You're driving," Stu says. "I'm going to need to have a drink after all."

"Oh," I reply, straightening back to full height. We'd talked about this. We'd talked at length and I thought he was on the same page. We agreed that he was going to cut right back on his drinking. It was that—he says—that caused the affair in the first place.

They were on a night out after a hard week. They'd lost a child to smoke inhalation. Stu never coped well with the losses. He wanted to save everyone. That's why I fell in love with him. The team went to the pub. They needed it. They needed the comradery. They needed each other. I was fine with it. I just wanted my husband to heal, that's why I never had a problem with him going out with the lads. That was before I knew about her. Lucy. I can say her name. I'll have to see her face in about half an hour so I can say her name in my mind.

Lucy was all over him. At least, that's what I imagine. Stu hasn't gone into detail, he'd just told me that it started that night. They kissed. The next day they laughed it off to the drink and the hard work, and they got on with their lives. But while I was taking care of our child—and trying to edit for my clients on the side, basically spending all my time working—Stu started lying about his shifts. He was seeing her instead. And that's when they developed feelings for each other.

"It's my night. I need to have a drink to celebrate. You don't mind do you? We won't be staying late, we have Emma with us." He ruffles our daughter's hair and smiles down at her. Emma beams up at him.

"Why don't I stay at home with Emma and then you have all night to get pissed?" I snap.

Stu doesn't react for a moment. He's been allowing me some grieving time after I found out about him and Lucy. But it's been six months now. We've still not made love. I only started allowing him back in our bed a month ago. I know he's waiting for me to get over it and move on. He's waiting for forgiveness, but I don't know if I can give it.

Stu gently takes hold of both arms. He looks me dead in the eye. "I want you both there to see this, because I want you to see I can be a good man." Then he bends down and picks up Emma, planting a big kiss on her cheek.

Oh, and the words pull on my heart so hard that I could cry, again, right there. I'm lost in his blue eyes, like I was the first time we met. I've never met anyone with eyes so blue and yet so warm and inviting. He's still handsome, even after the marriage and the child. He hasn't lost even the smallest bit of his sparkle. Whereas I've lost mine, and that's not me being negative, it's real. I've lost it, and I can feel that I've lost it, but I don't know how to get it back.

"Come on," he says. "You prefer driving anyway." He glances at his watch. "Hannah, we're really late."

I snap out of it. He's right, we have to go. Stu carries Emma down the drive as I lock the front door. It takes a couple more minutes to get her into the car seat before I make my way around to the driver's seat.

"Shit," Stu says, pulling on his seatbelt. "I can't believe it. I'm going to miss it."

"You're not," I say, pulling out of the drive.

It's a cold November, and the night is dark. I flick on the headlights and pull out of the drive with a screech of the tyres.

"Hannah the badass!" Stu exclaims approvingly.

But I take the edge off the accelerator so as not to go above the speed limit as we pass our neighbours. We chose well when it came to houses. It was just before the prices went sky-high. We got a good sized house in a sought after neighbourhood. We almost had it all, but then Stu ruined it with Lucy. I shake my head, trying to force the thoughts out of my head. But the truth is, I'm on edge about tonight. It'll be the first time I see her since I found out and it makes my stomach churn.

"Come on, Han, put your foot down."

I take a right at the end of the street towards the town centre. Parking is a nightmare around the City Hall where the event is being held. It's already 7:30 and the event started at 7. Sure, there'll be time for drinks and chatting at the beginning, but Stu can't miss his own presentation. I change gear and try to speed up a little. I've never been a confident driver. I was overcautious enough to get a minor for slowing down when I should have sped up during my driving test. I've never taken risks, I don't live like that. Whereas Stu, he loves adrenaline.

"I'm hurrying, okay, I can't do much more."

"I'm going to miss it." He lets his head fall back onto the headrest. "The one good thing that's happened this year and I'm going to miss it."

"The one good thing?" I say, aghast. "What about the things your daughter has done this year. Don't they count? What about teaching your daughter how to kick a ball, taking her swimming, helping her paint pictures?"

"You know what I mean, Han. Don't make a big deal

of it."

"At least you have one good thing happen. It's been a year of nothing but shit for me this year."

Stu's jaw tenses. "I know, you've told me. It's not like I can go back and erase it all, can I? It's just you won't fucking move on."

Emma starts crying in the back seat. I cluck my tongue. "Now look what you've done."

"Yeah because everything's my fault, isn't it? I cause everything to go wrong." His voice raises a fraction.

I grip the steering wheel, my fingernails digging into the leather. I press down on the accelerator and take a sharp left. It's starting to rain and the road is slippery. I can't help it. I start to cry. I try so hard not to, but all I can think about is our wedding day and how it felt so full of promises, so full of wonderful opportunities to come. Where did they all go?

"Hannah, for fuck's sake, you're going to miss the turning."

"What?" I'm pulled back to reality, with a screaming child in the back and a husband shouting next to me.

I swerve to the right, barely able to see the turning through my tears and the rain. The car swings around, but the water on the road makes it slide out beneath me. I don't see the headlights until it's too late. The van smashes into the side of the car, breaking the windows and scattering glass everywhere. The air bag hits me in the face, and pain explodes from my nose.

The car comes to a screeching halt. Completely bewildered, I search around me, trying to work out what has happened. The car is trapped between a van, and a barrier on the side of the road. Then I turn to my left and see the blood.

HANNAH

"They say you've not been taking your pills." James regards me beneath his heavy lids. My brother always had a habit of appearing bored when he was talking to you. For a while, I just saw it as his shtick. I never believed he really was bored. But when we drifted apart, it began to annoy me. I felt like it was real.

"You got fat," I reply, letting my gaze drift down to his beer belly. His face has expanded, too. He's not obese, but James was always pretty vain about his looks, so him putting on weight is a big deal.

"Turns out you can't eat what you want when you're forty," he says with a shrug. "Jill doesn't mind."

"I bet she does," I say. "She just won't tell you."

He laughs. "Probably."

I adjust my weight on the hospital bed. I hardly remember them bringing me in. There wasn't much they could do except administer a sedative to calm me down. Panic attacks are more complicated than a broken arm or an infection. It's my mind that needs to heal, not my body.

"Are you going to tell me what's been going on?" He leans forward and places a fist under his chin, squashing the loose flesh there.

The softness of his words is what catches me off guard. I want to cry again. The tears prick at my eyes. I can only shake my head.

"The police are letting you off with a caution. That's good."

I'd already been given the lecture from PC Baker. I knew this. I wipe a tear away from my eye and try to avoid James's gaze. Not since the accident have I felt so low. Every part of me is tired of fighting. I'm so exhausted from trying to just continue.

"Can you take me home?" I ask.

"Of course I can," he says. "But I want to know what's been happening first. Even when you went through the breakdown you never hurt anyone. You're not a violent person, Hannah. I don't understand why you would attack anyone."

"It's complicated."

"The police told me that you've got some sort of obsession with the family across the street. You've been stalking them on Facebook and phoning them. None of this is anything like you. I don't understand."

"And you don't have to understand. Just take me home."

"Is that a good idea? You're only a few feet away from them. Why don't you come and stay with me for a few days. We'll get you back on your pills. Once they've kicked in, and you're all evened out, you can go home."

"No. I won't be a zombie again. That's what they do to me. They stop me feeling anything. I don't want that anymore. I want to remember. I deserve to keep feeling the pain after what I did." I drag my fingernails along my jeans, pressing hard into my flesh.

"No, you don't deserve that. It's time to move on now. It could have happened to anyone. I mean it. We all break the speed limit sometimes. You didn't even take the full blame in court. The driver of the van admitted not looking both ways. It is not all your fault." He sighs in frustration because we've had this conversation before. James has always tried to let me off, but I won't have it. I killed my husband and baby daughter. Their blood is on my hands.

"I want to go home. James, please take me. I promise I won't go anywhere near the Masons. I just want to go home."

But James is in his own world, shaking his head. "They have what you might have had. You'd have that family now. That's what it is, isn't it?" He comes back to the room, meeting my gaze with his hooded eyes. "You have to see them every day, living the life that was meant for you."

I put my head in my hands in time to catch the tears that fall. The sobs rack through my body, but I manage to speak in a high-pitched, squeaky voice. "They don't treasure it. They're throwing it all away. And I know they are hurting her."

* * *

Every nurse seems to stare at me as we leave the hospital. Every patient or visitor does, too. When we pass the canteen and gift shop on the way out, more faces focus on us. I hang my head, sure that they can see my guilt written across my face. This has been my life since the accident. I'm the woman who killed her family in one split second. I had everything, then the glass smashed and I had nothing. Now they see me. Broken, hollowed out, pathetic. I'm the woman stalking her neighbours out of jealousy and spite. I'm dirty. Disgusting.

Whatever they gave to keep me calm wasn't very strong, because I can already feel the spreading tightness in my chest as we make our way through the hospital carpark. I know what's coming next. I know what I'm expected to do.

"I don't know if I can." I take a deep breath and slow down.

James puts a hand on my arm. "It's a ten minute drive. It's me, Han. You know I'm a good driver. I'll take it steady, and you can sit and close your eyes the entire time. Ten minutes, that's all."

Ten minutes. I can get through ten minutes.

I don't know the make of James's car. I never remember the badges anymore, they all blur into one. When I'm walking down the street, I stare straight ahead. I never look at the road, because I know how mundane the road was where my daughter died. I know it could have been any street at any time. That's how it works.

He has to open the door for me, but I pull on my seat belt. I run my finger over the dashboard, feeling the grooves. The smell of the car is pleasant for a moment, and a happy memory flashes in my mind, one where Emma is laughing in the back seat. Stu is driving, but he glances in the rearview mirror to smile at her. I'm smiling at Stu, enjoying him being a good dad. Then I hear the smash of glass ringing in my ears and that hard knot in my chest comes back.

"Deep breaths, Han," James slams his door and pulls on his seatbelt. "You can close your eyes if you like."

"If I close my eyes I'll see it again."

James's purses his lips and lets out a small sigh, whether it's of frustration or disapproval, I'm not sure. James is a straight-up guy. He keeps moving so that he doesn't have to think or feel. Everything has been in an orderly fashion for him. He got his GCSE's, then an apprenticeship, then a job at a warehouse, then a fiancé, then a manager's job, then a wife, then a kid, and so on. If anything bad happens to him—like the death of our parents, six months apart, both heart attacks from a bad lifestyle—he focusses on the practical side. He organises the funeral, arranges the will. He did the same for Stu and Emma's deaths. He got to work on all the legalities so I had time to grieve. But now he thinks my grieving time is over and I should be moving on. I should have moved on a long time ago. He would have.

I'm the emotion to his practical side. I was the one who acted out after our parent's divorce. James focussed on his apprenticeship. I was the one who screamed bloody murder when our parents were taken too soon. I'm not made of the same stuff as him. Somehow all the logic went into James and all emotion poured into me. No matter how hard I try to stay in control, that emotion flows out until I'm a nervous wreck.

I flinch when the ignition starts. I suck in a breath when the car begins to move. James bites his lower lip, clearly annoyed with me, probably rolling his eyes in his mind and wondering why the hell I overreact to everything.

A wave of nausea washes over me as James drives out of the car park. My left leg begins to shake, and I have to take long, slow breaths to try and calm my heart.

"Are you all right?" James asks.

I nod. *I can get through this.* I could take my eyes off the road, but I don't let myself. I have to face up to it. I have to watch the cars through the glass and realise that 99% of people get to where they're going safe and sound without a collision.

"You're doing well, Hannah." James actually sounds impressed, which is a rarity.

The rest of the time goes so slowly that I find myself counting down the seconds. If I've made it sixty seconds, I can make the next ninety seconds. If I stay here in my seat without freaking out for two minutes, I can make the next three minutes. For some reason, the last ten seconds are the hardest. That's when I end up staring across at the Masons' house.

"Is that them?" James asks.

"Yeah, that's them."

"The house seems normal enough."

"Something is going on behind those closed doors. I just know it is."

"You have to let this go," he says it in a firm but soft way.

"I know," I say. And it almost feels like I mean it. At least, it seems to be enough to persuade James, because his shoulders drop, and his face relaxes.

Edith's curtains aren't the only ones twitching when I leave the car. It takes me a couple of attempts to get out of the car. James has low seats, and my legs have lost their strength. He shuts the door for me and I pass him my keys so he can open the house. I can't help but glance at number 72. Matt and Laura stand in the window with frowns on their faces. April is in her room upstairs. She smiles down to me.

"I'll put the kettle on," James says.

He opens the living room window before going into the kitchen. The house smells of stale whiskey. Or that could just be me. As I scan the room, it dawns on me that this house isn't as safe as I think it is. It isn't a haven, it's my jail. I've been punishing myself over the last few years because I didn't believe that I deserved to live. It wasn't losing Stuart and Emma that ruined my life, it was what came after. I allowed myself to shrink. Like a tortoise disappearing into its shell, I confined myself to this house so that I didn't have to face the world.

"Cuppa?" James holds out the mug, and I realise I've been standing staring at the walls while James has made the tea.

I take the mug by the handle and sip the hot liquid. "Stuart bought me this mug. I always put it at the back of the cupboard so I don't see it every day."

"Sorry, I saw it and I remembered that it used to be your favourite. I thought it might bring you some comfort."

"It does, actually. I didn't think it would, but you're right."

"Hannah, why didn't you call me? When things started getting on top of you, all you had to do was call me and I would come to check you're all right. You know that. I'm only an hour away."

I can't think of any answer that's both the truth and valid. "I stopped looking outward."

"I can see that. You don't leave this place very often, do you? Have you even got any friends?" James sighs. "I thought by giving you some space that you would go out there and start to move on. You were leaning on me so much after the funeral that I thought it would help. But I went away for too long, didn't I? I..." He stops talking and takes a gulp of tea before wincing at the heat.

James settles onto the sofa, but I stand. I don't want to

touch anything in this house anymore. For the first time I see my furniture with fresh eyes. These are the things with which I've surrounded myself during my self-imposed house arrest. That coffee table is from a fake life. That chair is a lie. Those ornaments are symbols of this phoney life I've constructed. All of it reminds me of the crippling anxiety I've developed through sheer will to be punished. This is all a product of my guilt. Finally, I realise it. My guilt isn't an emotion, it's a living, breathing thing, suffocating me until I'm a husk.

"You had a life to live," I say. "I don't blame you, you know. I wasn't good company. I frightened your kids with my constant crying, and poor Jill didn't quite know what to do with me."

"I have more to apologise for," James says. "I should have done more when we were children. When it was bad... when they were fighting and—"

"Let's not talk about that." I move over to the sofa. I want to be close to my brother. "I want to know how you are. How are the children?"

Two hours later, after James has been to the shop and bought me food, and after he's showed me all the good TV shows I've been missing while I've been obsessed with the Masons, James leaves. For the first time in a long while, my house feels empty after he's gone. For so long now I've felt nothing but uncomfortable with anyone else in my space, but now I just want him back so we can carry on talking. I don't want to stop. I'm tempted to ring up a PPI claim salesman and talk his ear off for an hour. Instead, I check all my doors and windows are locked, then I go upstairs, and get in the bath.

I know I should be worried about my stay in jail and the

trip to the hospital, but I'm not. I'm even glad it happened. I lived through it. I made it out of the house for a night. I travelled in a car, and I talked to a whole range of people. None of those things killed me. I survived.

After my bath, I make a hot chocolate, slip into pyjamas, pull the curtains shut, and open the photo albums I'd kept hidden away in a box. The first picture almost takes my breath away. I'm tempted to close the album, put it back inside its box, Sellotape it shut, and hide it under the bed out of sight, like a spider left under a glass for someone else to deal with. But I don't. I run my finger over the picture instead, imagining what her soft skin really felt like when she was alive. The photograph is of a smiling man holding a chubby baby. Emma was three months when this picture was taken, and her cheeks had reached that chubby cuteness that all babies should have.

I close my eyes and remember her smell. It comes to me so fast and so vivid that I can hardly believe it. Sweetness and warmth, not unlike my hot cocoa, but with a tinge of baby sick. Maybe one day I will forget that smell. That day will hurt, but I will live through it. Knowing that feels very strange.

Each page is a beautiful torture. More than once, I have to close my eyes and concentrate on my breathing. But if I can get through one picture, I can get through the next, and before I know it, I've been through all of my photo albums, and I have cherished every memory.

I close the last page, wipe tears from my eyes and stand up to take my empty mug through to the kitchen. I chose the mug Stuart bought me on purpose this time. It's only a silly one with my name on the side. He bought it as a stocking filler and put "love Emma" on the tag. It was our first Christmas with Emma and every present felt special. I rinse out the mug, promising myself that I will fix the tap this time. I walk back into the living room to pack the photo albums away. It's then that I notice the envelope on the doormat.

Even though I use the back door for coming and going, I've not got round to moving the letter box. The post is still delivered through the front door, which always gets my pulse racing if I'm sat on the sofa. There's a boot print over the envelope, so I know this was delivered before James brought me home. But there's no stamp, which is odd. I bend down and retrieve the letter. The address is handwritten in a loose style, covering most of the cream envelope. Whoever delivered this did so by hand. They've been at my house.

LAURA

"How could you?" I want to throw the glass at him. If it hadn't cost me so much money, I'd throw the laptop at him, too. Instead, I carry on scrolling through all the messages instead. Some of them make me sick. "They're barely legal, Matt. It's disgusting. You're a pig." I gulp down the rest of the wine, trying to build up the courage to scroll through more of them. I'm not sure I can, or that I want to. "How could you?"

"Oh shut up. Why don't you just go to work like always? Just leave me here, your domestic slave to do all the shit you don't want to do."

I'm on my feet so fast that the laptop slides onto the carpet, landing with a thud. "I work so we have money. I provide for us. You don't mind spending it, do you? I bet you take your whores out for dinner with all this money I'm earning. What is it, Matt? A little afternoon delight while I'm at work?"

Matt shakes his head. "You've been poisoned by that bitch across the road. It's flirtation, that's all it is. These students, they have bags of cash from their rich mummies and daddies. All I'm trying to do is charm them so they'll hire me. I'm trying to get work so *I* can pay my way. Do you think I enjoy living off your handouts? No fucking way."

"You should have thought about that before you quit your job." I walk across the room, staring at Hannah's house. The place is empty after her arrest. I hope she never comes back. I never want to see her face again. As it is, I'll forever remember her bloodshot eyes as she attacked my husband. I'll never forget the absolute hatred she exuded when accusing him of hurting April.

"You supported me, Laura. Don't try to pretend you didn't. You said that we would get by and that you wanted me to be happy."

"That was before I found out what makes you happy is sleeping with women fifteen years younger."

"I haven't slept with anyone." Matt leans back against the sofa and runs his hands through his hair. He laughs. "It's not like I've even been sleeping with you."

I make a disgusted noise. "You're a cliché. Poor Matt, whose wife is so knackered when she gets back from work that she doesn't put out anymore. Poor sex deprived Matt, who has to hit on eighteen-year-olds to get his fix. You're disgusting. Look at you. You're ridiculous. You're thirty-eight and you're wearing a V-neck T-shirt. You think those muscles make you more attractive, but you're repulsive."

"At least I haven't let myself go. At least I care about how I look—"

"Shut up. Liar! Just shut up."

The room goes silent. I move away from the window, pick up the laptop and place it on the armchair.

"We need to stop arguing," I say.

"We'll stop arguing when you stop believing the mentally ill woman across the street," Matt says bitterly.

"No," I say, letting out a heavy sigh. "We need to stop arguing for April. Don't you see? This isn't about us. It's about her."

Matt's eyes narrow. "What do you mean?"

HANNAH

I stare at the unopened letter in my hands. There's the sound of a door slamming, and I can't help but stare out of the window. Matt Mason opens his car door, slings a bag into the passenger seat, then gets in and drives away. I stand there open mouthed. Is this it? Has Laura thrown him out? This means that I've won. I've actually won against him.

The door to number 72 opens again, but this time it's Laura. She strides across the street, hugging her body, wrapped in a thick cardigan despite the warm weather. I step away from the window and close the curtains. The unopened letter gets shoved into my pocket without thinking. When Laura knocks on the door, my muscles clench.

"I need to talk to you," Laura says. "It's important." The letter box opens, and one eye appears through the gap. "I need to talk to you about Matt, and about April. Come on, Hannah, I'm not mad at you anymore. I need to find out what's been going on."

"I can't. The police have told me to stay away from you. I can't be seen talking to you."

"Then let me in before anyone notices. Please, this is about April. I need to know my daughter is safe."

I think of my promise to James. He'll be so mad at me when he finds out. But then I've been disappointing James for a long time. I let out a long breath before opening the door.

"I have to be quick, I left April alone," she says.

"I thought you didn't believe me." I shut the door and move into the centre of the room so we're not too close.

Laura sinks into the sofa. Her legs almost fold in on themselves. The Laura I first met is almost completely gone. "I don't know what to believe anymore. The police say you have issues and that you've become obsessed with us, but I look at you and I'm not sure that's true. You were so nice to me when I came to yours. Why did you keep everything to yourself? You could have told me."

"I was going to. But it's not something you blurt out. At first I thought you knew about the police and were trying to figure out if it was me who called. But then I realised you didn't even know, and I wanted to say, but you left really quickly."

"Tell me everything," Laura says. Her red-ringed eyes are open wide, and slightly wild.

I sit down in the chair nearest the window and I tell Laura everything, from April's sign, to Edith's observations, even what I saw in the pub. I tell her about April appearing in my garden, and the sock-puppet Facebook accounts.

"My God." Laura places a hand on her mouth. "How have I missed all this?"

"Do you think Matt is hurting April?" I ask. It makes me feel nauseous asking a wife that question.

Laura is still for what feels like a long time. "I've been asking myself that question all day. A few months ago, I would have laughed it away. But Matt has become so angry recently. He's like a different person." She shakes her head. "I didn't think him capable of cheating a few months ago."

"Well, he's gone now. You're safe, and April is safe."

But Laura's eyes are glazed over and she's staring at a spot on the wall, barely even acknowledging my existence. "We adopted her, you know. We'd been trying for a baby of our own, but it wasn't happening. She was eight at the time. We met with her a few times before the adoption, and she was such a beautiful little girl. I fell in love with her straight away, but Matt was harder to convince. Then, one afternoon, we sat with her in the playroom of the foster home she was staying in, and Matt read her a story. It was like falling in love with him all over again. He was so gentle and kind with her." Laura wipes away a tear and I pass her some tissues. "She really warmed to him. She'd smile as soon as he walked into a room. We'd not been getting on too well for a while. Matt was unhappy at work. He'd missed out on a promotion and he was getting frustrated with being passed over so often. April was the missing piece to make us whole again, and for a while, it really worked.

"She made me happy to come home again. I'd look forward to making her dinner, brushing her hair. But she was so quiet when we first adopted her. She wasn't like other eight- year-old girls. She didn't love Barbies and have sleep-overs. She wasn't interested in clothes or nail polish. As the months—and then years—went on, I found it harder and harder to talk to her. But Matt was always so great with her. He made her laugh. They played video games together and cooked together. For some reason, she never bonded with me. I've always loved her like she's my own, but sometimes I would look at April, and I would feel like she didn't feel the same way. I was always Laura to her. It took me years to get her to call me Mum.

"But then I knew about her past, and I knew how difficult it would be for April to open up to us. She had a bad start in life. She lost her parents very young. By all accounts, her parents weren't good people. They treated her badly. That was one of the reasons why I wanted to give her a happy home. Well, I've failed at that.

"When Matt left work, things got even worse. Matt thought he'd find work as a personal trainer right away. But he was inexperienced, and he didn't have the connections he needed. I paid for one course after the other, thinking that Matt would get it together and we'd soon have a second source of income. But that didn't happen, we had to sell our house and move further out of the city. Matt ended up a house husband, and really hated it. He's been getting more and more angry, and I think... I think he might be taking steroids, too."

"Has he ever hit you?" I ask.

"Yes... and no... He doesn't smack me around, if that's what you mean." Laura's tone is hard, defensive. "But he's been a bit... forceful with me sometimes."

"I saw him slap you," I remind her.

"That's been the worst," she says. "And I think it's all from the steroids. It's not really him. He's a mess. We both are."

"Tell me you're not staying with him," I say. "Tell me you're not going to let him back. Not after everything I just told you about April, about the bruises on her arms."

"Look, you can't trust April. I know all you see is this vulnerable child, but she's not, okay? She's a liar. She's been making stuff up for years. At first it was white lies, like eating all the Christmas chocolate, or ruining an art display at school. Then it got worse. She told us she was being bullied. So we went down to the school, and we yelled and kicked off at the teachers, only to find out that she is the bully and has been nasty to some of the other girls at school. She's a troubled girl." Laura rubs her palms against her jeans as though getting the sweat off them.

"But surely, this is different," I say. "You know Matt has a temper, and he's alone with her all day. If she annoys him, he could easily snap."

Laura chews on her bottom lip and stares out of the window towards her own house. "It's more complicated than you know."

"She's still a child," I say. "And children shouldn't be brought into a dysfunctional home."

"Are you judging me?" Her eyes flash.

I hold up my hands to placate her. "No. I'm really not. I mean... you need to resolve your relationship issues with Matt. Either he needs to change, or you need to throw him out. And you need to be sure he's not hurting her, because it's not fair to that child." I hold back a sob.

Laura stands up when there's the sound of a car moving along Cavendish Street. My heart sinks when I see Matt getting out with his bag.

"I have to go," she says.

I watch Laura through the window. She's an odd woman. I didn't realise at first, but now I see it. Despite her initial friendliness, and despite her opening up about April and Matt, there is an aloofness about her. And, worse, I don't feel like I can trust her. Perhaps it's that frozen smile and the lack of warmth she exudes, especially when talking about her daughter. She doesn't seem to put April first, and I can't figure out why any mother would behave like that. Seeing her go back into that house with Matt, I know something is still wrong. Then I remember the letter.

As soon as I hear the slam of the front door, I want to escape. They're back. I watched from my bedroom window. And now the arguing has started already. I hurry into the bathroom and lock the door. I don't want to take any chances this time, not after last time. The screaming gets worse. I can't bear it. I just want it to stop. I put my hands over my ears and the tears start to fall.

When the footsteps start coming up the stairs, I sink down onto the floor next to the bath. My heart is racing. Please don't find me. Please don't find me.

I want this to end.

HANNAH

I crumple the note into my hand. I'm on edge, razor sharp. Everything has come into focus now.

I can't believe the contents of the letter, yet somehow I always knew. This is more than my obsession with the Masons, now. It's more important than that.

Laura Mason has taken her husband back, and that means something.

It takes me less than a minute to make up my mind.

I know what to do.

LAURA

The fighting stopped almost as soon as it began. I think we exhausted ourselves. Then Matt went upstairs to speak to April. I've been glugging down wine ever since, imagining Hannah's judgemental eyes as she questioned me. *Has he ever hit you?* I didn't answer quite honestly. I didn't tell her everything.

I set down my wine and hurry upstairs. Matt and April are talking in hushed tones behind her bedroom door. I swing it open and the two them turn towards me with guilty expressions on their faces.

"I was telling April how everything is going to be all right now," Matt says, stretching his grin a little too wide.

"Is it?" I reply. Nervous energy pulses through me, making my breathing laboured. I close and unclose my fists, trying to stay calm. "April, I think it's time for you to go to bed now. Okay?"

"Can I get a glass of water first?" she asks.

I nod once, and move out of her way as she leaves the room. I watch her as she goes downstairs. Ever since we adopted her, I've always had this niggling paranoia that she doesn't like me. No matter what I do, or what I buy her, she never opens up to me. But maybe that's why. Kids know a phoney when they see one, and April can see the regret all over my face. I regret adopting her. It didn't fix anything, it made things worse. It ruined my relationship with Matt, and it pushed me towards my job as an escape.

But I *do* love her. Is that possible? To regret a child's existence but also love them? What kind of monster am I? What kind of *mother*? I should face facts. I was never supposed to be a mother, and I'm not one now. I'm the temporary guardian of a girl who will probably leave as soon as she's old enough.

"You shouldn't have said that to her," Matt says.

I don't answer, instead I walk out of the room and leave him there. April passes me on the stairs, with her long hair trailing half across her face so I can't see her expression. I never know what she's thinking.

"Laura." Matt takes hold of my upper arm and pulls me downstairs. "Are you listening to me? You can't act like that around her. We need to be united."

"I told you earlier everything that I needed to say. This marriage is over, Matt. You shouldn't be here."

His face contorts. At first he grimaces as though in pain, then his face tightens as though he's furious. I back away from him, my insides squirming. It's like a nest of snakes are moving through my intestines. I scan the living room exits, wondering if I have time to run. Matt's shoulders rise, his muscles bulge as he clenches his fists. His jaw starts to work, and I can see that he's grinding his teeth.

"Matt," I say, changing tone to a soothing, quiet one. "It's what's best for us all. Just give us some time, okay?"

"You're talking about throwing me out of my fucking home."

I back away, bumping into the armchair, tripping over the laptop charger. I'm a stumbling, bumbling fool letting my husband bully me. My heart thumps in my chest, causing my pulse to thud in my ears. Every time I take a step back, Matt narrows the space between us, until he only needs to reach out with his hands to grab me by the throat.

"Dad, you should go."

Matt spins around at the sound of April's voice. I take advantage of the distraction, hurrying away from him and towards April. My husband is almost dumbfounded by April standing against him. He blinks before shaking his head. The red mist seems to have cleared, and his fists unclench. Even still, I flinch as he barges past us, and flings open the front door, not bothering to close it. As the car screeches away, I close the door and lock it.

"It's for the best," I say to April.

She stands there for a second in her panda bear pyjamas, and I open my arms for her to fall into them. But April doesn't come to me for comfort. As she walks away, my arms fall to my sides. I've failed.

HANNAH

Timing is everything. If I don't do this right, it'll mess everything up. I spent all night waiting. Most of the morning, waiting. I watched Matt Mason leave the house last night. I lay awake listening to the night, expecting to hear his car come back, but it never did. Laura Mason left this morning, too. She was in her smart work clothes again. I listened by the window as she talked to April on the street. I heard April ask to stay at home, then I heard Laura snap at her, and tell her that she had to stay with Laura's friend for the day. Then they got in the car together.

I had to wait some more. Timing is everything.

When I know it's right, I open my back door and hurry along the alleyway. Edith is out with her daughter today, I saw her get picked up. That's good. I can do without Edith watching my every move.

The keys feel strange in my hand. They're warm from my body heat, but they're hard and unyielding against my flesh. Today is as good as any to do this. The weather is perfect: not too hot, not too cold. The sun is shining, but there are little fluffs of clouds covering it, so that it's not too bright. It's a typically muted English summer day. The stifling heatwave is about done.

I take a deep breath. This week I have stayed in a police cell, been to hospital, and been in my brother's car. They were the hillocks on the way to this mountain. They were training me for this moment. I put the key into the car door.

My Ford hasn't moved for a year. After the accident, my brother insisted on making me buy a car. I had some money from the life-insurance and the sale of our house. With some of that money I bought the car and the small house I live in now. To pay my bills I use Stu's savings, and my money from the editing. I don't have many. I kept up the car insurance, thinking that one day I would get into my car and drive away. I don't eat a lot. I hardly ever buy clothes, unless I need new underwear or jeans. I don't spend much money on the house, and my heating and electric is manageable. I keep convincing myself that all of it means I'm getting by, I'm surviving. But am I living?

The door opens with a click. I have no idea if it will even start. Do I remember how to drive? I slide into the seat and close my eyes. Then I check all around me. I check for insects, for litter, for any kind of distraction that will stop me from driving this car out of Cavendish Street and to where I need to go. When I put the key in the ignition, my heart is pounding, and my chest is tight.

It won't start, and then you can stop all this nonsense.

I'm almost willing myself to fail before I've even begun. I rotate the key and listen to the engine try to tick over. It makes a juddering screech before stopping altogether. I let out a long exhale and slump against the wheel. That's it. I tried.

But determination forces me to carry on. I twist the keys again, my heart thumping away, adrenaline coursing through my veins. *Chug-chug-chug-chug-ch-ch.* I remember how Stuart used to rev the engine when the car wouldn't start in winter. Tentatively, I apply pressure to the accelerator. *Vrooom-vroom-chug-chug-chhhrrrr-brrrr.* My heart soars and my stomach sinks when it happens. This is real, then. I'm really going to do it.

My fingers tighten against the steering wheel. This is my moment of bravery, my heroic act. I've made it into my car, and I'm going to save someone. I'm changing everything, because of what was written in that note. But I don't feel like a hero when I let down the handbrake, slowly release the clutch, and begin to drive away. My hands shake as I change gear. I creep down the street, dreading passing cars. I can't drive the entire way this speed, I know that. I have to go faster, but as the speedometer needle goes up, my heart beat quickens.

Make it to the end of the road. Put on your indicator. Turn right. Keep driving down the road. Ignore the cars coming the other way. Go faster.

I bargain with myself at every moment. If I can get through this bend, I can turn at the cross roads. It's less than a five minute drive, but it feels epic, like a three hour film or a ten year war.

I see her right away, and I pull into the verge as slowly and carefully as I can. She has a backpack on her shoulders, and is standing on the grass waiting for me, shadowed by the woods behind her. This is where she said she would be. She wanted to be away from the house. Seeing her makes my heart beat faster. *What if I'm making a mistake?* She opens the door and gets in.

"Thank you," she says, with shining eyes.

"It's going to be okay, April. I'm going to take you to the police station and they'll help you." Seeing her, talking to her, I know this is the right thing to do.

I couldn't ignore the letter. She wrote to me, telling me how it was both Laura and Matt who hurt her. As I read the letter, I thought of nothing but how cold Laura had appeared when talking about her daughter. She barely even seemed to like April, and was far more upset by Matt's cheating. When she told me that April lied, and that I couldn't trust her, I thought it was really strange that she wasn't taking things more seriously. The letter clarified everything. Laura gets drunk, yells at April, and hits her, too.

What kind of a person would I be if I left her to that? When I saw Laura leave this morning, it confirmed everything for me. What kind of a mother goes to work the morning after her husband has been thrown out? Someone like that doesn't deserve to have a child if she doesn't love them. Not when there are those who have had their children taken away from them.

"You're going to be fine, April, I promise," I say as I drive away from Cavendish Street.

LAURA

Almost as soon as I get to work, I know I've made a huge mistake. I should have stayed at home with April. But when I woke up that morning, April was downstairs eating cereal, and I realised that I had nothing to say to her. I couldn't think of anything that would make things better, I couldn't think of anything to say that would comfort her. I felt like such a failure, that I did the most cowardly thing I've ever done in my life. I took her to my nearest uni friend's house, a few miles away from Cavendish Street, and I left her there.

I haven't spoken to Jen for a few months. Not since Matt insulted her husband's new car. Matt was jealous, so he spent the entire evening getting progressively more drunk, and making rude remarks about how much money they had, and how they've wasted it on the car. He then made a horrible comment about Jen not being able to have children, and how she should get a job instead of being a house wife.

"Women who aren't mothers shouldn't stay at home all day and do nothing. They should at least go to work."

My artist friend took offense to that. She'd sold a few paintings. Rob earned more than enough for the both of them, and that allowed Jen to stay at home and paint. But to Matt that was selfish if you didn't have children. They were depriving the world of their offspring. I felt sick to hear him say those things.

I'm lucky enough that Jen doesn't often hold a grudge, and I knew she hadn't seen April for a long time. I knew she would want to see her, especially when I told her I'd kicked Matt out of the house. She actually breathed a sigh of relief before pulling me into a huge bear hug. She didn't say anything bad about him, and I love her for it, but I could see it on her face.

Not even an hour into work, the phone rings, and it's Jen.

"I don't want you to freak out," she starts.

"What's happened?" I'm sitting up straighter in my chair. I chew nervously on the lid of my biro.

"April has left. I'm sorry, Laura. I swear I only went into the studio for fifteen minutes. She was working on a sketch at the kitchen table, and I needed to wash some brushes before the paint hardened. I should have taken her into the studio with me. I'm so sorry."

I want to scream, but instead I say in a shaky voice. "It's okay. It's not your fault. I'll go home and check there. Then I'll ring Matt and see if she's with him."

I can tell Jen is crying. "I'm so sorry, Laura. I'll have a walk around the streets. There's a park ten minutes away. I'll see if she's there."

I hang up and try April's mobile, but it goes straight to voicemail, as I knew it would. April doesn't just take herself off to the park when she feels like it. She's not that kind of girl. This has something to do with me and Matt. Either she's gone home, or she's gone to Matt.

I hurry into my manager's office and tell them that I have to go. Then I rush down to the carpark and get in the car. Someone almost reverses into me as I pull out of the space. Or it could be that I almost drive into them, I'm in such a mess that I can't tell. I swing around the car park and out into the town centre. It's 11am and the traffic has died down, but there are many buses to watch out for. I take each corner a little too fast. I rush through amber as it's on the verge of turning red. More than one pedestrian shouts vague insults in my direction as I speed past them, their words lost on the wind.

I have to find her. I keep trying to imagine her at home, safe and sound. April knows how to get the bus on her own. She's a clever girl. I know Matt takes her on the bus into town sometimes. With the internet, it's far easier to plan how to get somewhere than it ever was when I was thirteen.

Cavendish Street feels even smaller than usual. It seems emptier, too, like there aren't as many parked cars as usual. I don't linger outside long enough to work out which cars are missing, I rush into the house and slam the door.

"April?"

The house is silent. I check every room before I try calling her again. There's no answer. I run my fingers through my hair and dial Matt's number. No answer. The house is silent as I let out another frustrated scream.

Where could she have gone? I make my way into April's room and close the door. I've put this off long enough. I need to find some answers. I drop to my knees, and start my search under the bed.

HANNAH

April can't sit still. Her neck is constantly craned as she gazes out of the window, or twists her body to see behind us. She moves around in her seat as though she's anxious and wants to be somewhere else. I start to wonder if I'm making a mistake. Is this kidnapping? If I let a thirteen- year-old into my car, am I committing a crime? I had thought that I was helping. That I was a hero. I have the letter in my bag, and I have April alone so she can tell the police what's happening. They didn't take me seriously before, but I didn't have any evidence then. Now I have April to tell them what's happening.

I'm *saving* her.

"Pull over," April says.

April's face is screwed up, like she's about to cry. She claws at her seatbelt, trying to take it off.

"But we're going—"

"Pull over!" April screams. The high-pitched nature of her desperation is so shocking and frightening that I miss a gear change and the car lurches. "Pull over, now!"

I swerve into the verge and slam on the brake. "What's going on, April? I thought you wanted to go to the police?"

The passenger door opens, and April hits the ground running. I watch her with a slack jaw, still for a moment, wondering what to do next. I watch April climb over the gate and into the field between the road and the woods. Then I shake my head, and cut the ignition. I can't let a troubled teenage girl run away into an empty field. I have to go and help her. I get out of the car and slam the door behind me, before following in April's footsteps and climbing over the gate.

"April!" I shout, but she's so fast that she's already disappeared into the field.

LAURA

The keys rattle from my shaking hands. It takes me three attempts to unlock the car door. I dropped the keys underneath the car in the first attempt. Then I climb into the seat, and rest my head on the steering wheel, trying to calm my heart.

I still feel sick. Every time I close my eyes, I see those images. It makes me nauseous to think that it was going on in my house and I never knew. Every woman thinks that they will know whatever is going on with their child. They're arrogant enough to think: *It'll never happen to me.* Or: *Why didn't that mother know? She should have known.* But now it has happened to me.

I've failed.

I put the key into the ignition and sit in the car for a few moments, trying to recollect my thoughts. I need to find April more than ever, but how am I going to do that? My fingers scroll through my phone, as though somehow the answer will magically appear.

But something magical does happen. I remember last

Christmas, when we bought April her new mobile. It was in hope that she might join in at school. All the girls liked to text or WhatsApp each other. I felt as though April was missing out on all that. But before we gave it to her, we put some restrictions on her phone. One of the things we installed was a GPS tracker so that if April lost it we could find it. Of course, it dawned on me then that I could use it to find her. But then April never really went out, so I never thought about it. I forgot all about it. Until now.

It takes me a while to figure out how to use the App. Matt was always better with technology. I used to let him do everything while I complained about things that didn't work. But then I find the little dot on the map, and I know exactly where she is.

HANNAH

I chase the red top April is wearing, watching how her black hair bobs up and down. The girl is fast. I have to sprint to keep up with her. I'm older, and slower, and desperately out of shape, but determination keeps me going. I can't let anything happen to her. Not when I'm so close to saving her.

When April begins sprinting towards the woods, I follow her, watching my feet so that I don't trip and fall. The ground is hard from the lack of rain. The grass is sparse and dry. My trainers kick up dust as I run. I've given up shouting her name. She knows I'm here, I know she can hear me. She doesn't want to answer. She wants me to follow.

What is she going to show me?

My chest tightens with panic. After everything April has been through, I'm scared of what it might be.

April begins to slow down. She glances behind her to check I'm still there, before disappearing between two trees. I hurry to follow her. April comes to a stop and looks back to check I'm still there. After meeting my gaze, she nods towards an outhouse.

I'd been watching April so intently that I hadn't seen it. It's half covered in branches and ivy, a little shed in the middle of the woods.

"What's in there?" I ask.

April backs away so I can go first. She doesn't say a word, and somehow that is worse for my imagination. I take a deep breath. I need to earn April's trust. My mouth goes dry as I take a step towards the shed. This could be a place her parents have brought her in order to hurt her. An isolated torture house. Sick images invade my mind. My stomach lurches. I feel sick. But I keep going. Whatever the reality is, it can't be as bad as what's in my head. My fingers are trembling as I reach for the door.

I turn back to her. "Do you want me to go in? Do you want to show me what's inside?"

April nods. Her eyes are open wide and vulnerable. There's a shine of emotion in her eyes, I think it is hurt, but it could just be the exhilaration from the run. She pulls at a thread on her red top, with her small shoulders hunched high. She's so young, so innocent. I almost can't bear to face the reality of what has been going on. But if I don't do it, who will?

I pull open the door. The inside of the outhouse is dark, and the place has an unused, musty smell. I scan the walls as I step in, trying to gauge what this place is. There's no blood, no shackles, no ominous weapons or torture devices. I let out a sigh of relief. I'm an idiot for letting my imagination run wild. There's some movement behind me as April follows me. I can't see what's in here. There doesn't seem to be much. But as my eyes adjust to the dark, I make out a lumpy shape in the far corner. I squint and lean forward to try and figure out what it is.

The air whistles. There's the sound of a thwack. I think it's surprise that I notice first, then that there's pain coming from the back of my head, then that whatever hit me has propelled me towards the ground. The side of my face hits the hard floor. I try to stay conscious, to keep my wits about me, but it's impossible. As the world changes to black, I feel the warmth of my blood dripping down my skull.

I can hear him downstairs bumping into the furniture. I know he's drunk. I don't even need to see him. Then the light goes on underneath the door, and Mum's footsteps patter along the hallway. I wait until she's down the stairs and then listen. I can usually tell when it's going to be bad. They start in hushed voices and get gradually louder until they're yelling. After the yelling, if it goes silent, I know what comes after silence. I know that soon I'll hear the sound of Mum begging him. Then he comes for me.

I jam a chair under my bedroom door handle. There's no time to run into the bathroom this time. I need somewhere else to hide. With my heart beating so hard I can hear it, I check the room for hiding places. There's under the bed. He'll check there first. Or in my wardrobe. Maybe if I make myself really, really small... Maybe he won't get in. Not with the chair jammed under the handle.

I scurry across the floor, open the wardrobe door and press myself all the way at the back, pulling the clothes around me. They're yelling at each other now. Mum will be telling him he's good for nothing. That he's a no good drunk. She'll be saying that he doesn't care about her. Then she drags me into it. He should be caring for his daughter. He should get a proper job and stop drinking all his money away. I'm working hard at school despite the bullying, despite everything.

Snap.

There's she goes. I hear the tumble onto the floor. He's hit his level. She's made him feel so inferior that he needs to prove he's a man.

I'm sorry. I'm sorry. Don't. Don't!

The begging. It always comes in a higher pitch, but it's gin-soaked and slurry. Mum drinks at home, Dad drinks in the pub. Then they meet in the middle and all hell breaks loose.

I hear him roar, and my blood goes cold. I hear the sound of his fist on her flesh. Then comes the silence I've been dreading. She's out. She's not fun to hurt anymore. He needs someone who will scream and beg.

It's my turn.

I bury my head in a thick woollen jumper to try and muffle the sound of my breathing. What if the chair won't hold? Maybe I didn't push it hard enough against the handle. My father is a large brute of a man. I'm a scrawny teenager. What if I haven't pushed it hard enough?

His footsteps travel slowly up the stairs. Either he's enjoying this moment of cat and mouse, or he's so drunk that he has to slow down. Or maybe it's a combination of the two. I think probably the latter. The creak of the top step tells me that's he's almost reached the hall.

I start to cry. The door won't hold against him. He's too strong. I imagine his feet under the door. Two blobs of black cutting off the yellow light. I bet he's still wearing his boots. Maybe he's even wearing his jacket. I wish that Mum would stay in bed when he comes back. Why can't she do that?

There's a thud as he slams his huge body into the door. I pull my knees up against my chest, making myself as small as I possibly can. I can almost feel the way his body hits the door. I feel the cold slap of the wood and the pain in his shoulder. The more he has to work to find me, the worse it will be. He cries out in frustration and starts kicking the door.

"There's no point hiding from me, Laura. I'm coming to get you."

HANNAH

A *crash of metal. The feeling of being thrown. Glass all over my lap. A tiny, broken body on the backseat.*
I wake up with a start, sucking in stale air. My nostrils are filled with the stagnant reek of an abandoned house. I open my eyes. This is not a house. I'm in a small, wooden shed. My body is bruised and aching, resting on a hard floor. For a moment I'm confused, but then I remember.

"April?"

There's no answer. I take in my surroundings. The shed is dark, but on one wall there are two very small slits of light around a piece of wood that resembles a slat designed to move forward and back. The floor is wooden, covered in the dust of old leaves and cobwebs. There are a few things on a shelf—a rusty tin, a pair of dusty binoculars, and what could be a hat. I try to stand so I can inspect the shelf, but it's then I realise my hands and feet are tied together with zip wire.

My head pounds. *I was hit.* But what was I hit with? I keep inspecting the shed for clues. Before I was hit I saw... The lumpy shape on the corner.

With my eyes adjusted to the dark, I can make out what the shape really is. When I realise, the panic hits me with such ferocity that I almost faint. The shape is Matt Mason slumped on his side. There's a trickle of dark liquid coming from the back of his head. His hands and feet are bound with zip ties. Someone hit him—like they hit me—before binding his hands and feet. His body is on his side, with his back slightly arched. I presume that April bound Matt where he fell after she hit him with the golf club.

The door opens, letting light into the tiny space. I wince and close my eyes. I don't want to, but my head is throbbing, and the light makes it worse. When the door swings shut, I open my eyes and see the person who has entered the shed. I let out a sigh of relief.

"April, quick, untie me," I say, holding out my hands.

But she doesn't move.

"Quickly, whoever did this might come back any..." My body goes cold when I see the smeared blood on her clothes, and the golf club in her hand. I don't understand at first. My first instinct is that she's hurt. An image of my own little girl broken and bloody pops into my mind.

April's laugh shakes the image out of my mind. "Haven't you figured it out yet?"

It only takes two of her short steps to reach me. She bends down and pushes the handle of the golf club into my hands. I just sit there and watch her with my jaw slack. April is wearing gloves. When did she put those on?

I think about her tears in the car; her insistence that I pull over. I think about how she ran through the fields, waiting as I caught up, before leading me here. Laura's voice pops into my mind, telling me about all of April's lies at school. Then I think about how April's mobile phone number is in my phone, how I'm in the middle of the woods with an injured man and a disturbed teenage girl.

She hit me. She lured me here and then she hit me over the head. She must have done the same with her father. But why?

"You've made a mistake," I say. "I'm older and stronger than you. I can stop whatever it is you're trying to do."

She removes the club from my hand, stands up to full height and examines the golf club with a thoughtful smile on her face, as though weighing up options in her mind. "Easy, I found you here standing over Daddy with the golf club, so I got a rock and hit you. Then I tied you up and called the police from my mobile phone." She drops the golf club, and pulls a phone out of her pocket.

I've gone beyond panic. What I feel now isn't anything like the fear I feel when I go to the shops or remember the accident. It's more like an acceptance. This is what is happening to me now, and there's nothing I can do to stop it. The nausea dissipates, leaving me with an unnatural sense of calm.

"Why?"

April smiles when she hears that one word. I get the impression she has been keeping this plan secret for such a long time that she relishes the chance to actually talk about it. I can't believe that this beautiful, young girl would even want to hurt anyone, let alone carry out such an intricate plan to do so.

"People always break their promises, don't they?" she says. Her voice is soft, almost gentle. It's the most I've ever heard her speak. The smile fades from her lips. Her eyes go hard. "All parents are the same. My biological parents were liars. They promised me that they wouldn't hurt me again. But they lied, because I'd come home from school, and Mum would be drunk. She never made anything for me to eat, so I would always have to make my own dinner. Then she'd bring her men over and I'd see her cheating on my dad like it was nothing. Later on they promised they wouldn't get divorced, but I knew better." She draws a line along the dust wooden floor of the hut. "I thought Laura and Matt were going to be different. I was actually happy when the social worker told me I'd be going with them. Matt told me he'd always be there for me, but I knew... I knew long before you figured it out. He's a cheater just like everyone else. And Laura, well, why have a kid if you've got no time for one? She doesn't care about anything but her job. She's never here. She says we'll do things together, but then she can't be bothered."

I try stretching out the zip ties with my hands and feet. Working them a fraction at a time, making small motions that April won't be able to see in the dim light.

"You're doing all this to get back at them?"

April nods. "People go unpunished, but they shouldn't. No one told off my mum when she bought cigarettes instead of food, or sent me to school in dirty clothes. She got away with slapping me when she was in a bad mood, or making me wash my mouth out with soap. People are supposed to be punished in this world. That's how it's supposed to work."

"And you think you're the right person to punish them, do you?"

She nods. The blank expression on her face makes me shudder.

"April, what happened to your biological parents?" I keep

talking because if I don't, she'll call the police. What can I say against a thirteen-year-old? My prints are on the club. I already have a history of stalking the Masons. Who will believe me?

"I burned them."

The words hang in the air. I'm stunned into silence.

April looks at me one last time, before she turns around and walks out of the shed. Before the door swings shut, I see her put the phone to her ear.

I don't have much time. I pull on the zip ties, trying to remember a YouTube video that went viral a few months ago, where a man broke out of zip ties by swinging his arms against a hard surface. But after a few attempts on my knees, I can tell I don't have the strength. Instead, I focus on the ties around my ankles. I slip off my trainers. The bulk of them made the ties wider when April applied them. If I contort myself I might be able to force the tie over my ankle. I grit my teeth as the rigid plastic digs into me, dragging down my socks and scraping the skin beneath. Sweat forms on my forehead as the ties draw blood from the top of my feet. I don't care. I ignore the pain. I have to get out.

But what am I going to do when I get away from her? Where am I going to go? No one will ever believe this story. It's too neat, too perfect. I'm the obvious prime suspect in Matt Mason's death. Who would ever suspect a thirteen-year-old girl with doe eyes and an innocent smile? I'll be on the run, living away from the world. I'll never be able to go to the police. I think about PC Baker with his long sighs and PC Ellis with her patronising tone.

I wince as the skin scrapes from the top of my foot. I take a deep breath and try again. The blood is becoming a lubricant for my feet. A little hope pushes me on. With one more try, I pull myself free of the bindings. I lean against the wall of the shed, catching my breath from the effort.

But I don't have long before I need to act. Outside, I can hear April sobbing down the phone. "My dad's dead! My dad's dead!"

My heart pounds, but I can stand now. That's something. There's not enough time to get the bindings off my hands, but now at least I can move.

Matt Mason lies still in the corner. I cast a glance at the golf club, considering it. But, no. I could never hurt her. Not even now. She's still a child. I have no choice but to outrun her.

The door of the hut swings open and April stands in the doorway. For the first time, I recognise panic in her eyes when she sees me on my feet. She looks towards the golf club, but I run at her before she even gets the opportunity. I use my full weight to slam into her on the way out, knocking her to the ground. My bare feet sting as I run over the rough terrain. I check behind me. April is back on her feet.

The bright sunshine illuminates the blood all over my shirt. It could be my blood, it could be Matt's, or even both. I'm a crazed, bound woman running through a field with my shirt soaked in blood.

Footsteps follow me. She's fast, but I have fear and adrenaline on my side. I have the will to survive for the first time in years. It's taken all this to realise that I want to live. I don't want to merely exist anymore, I truly want to live. It's only when my freedom is threatened that I come to my senses. I've been trying so hard to escape the past, that I hadn't realised I am right there stuck in the middle of it. I thought that moving out, boxing up all the memories, and putting the photograph albums away meant that I'd moved on. I was wrong.

There's a blur to my right. The red of April's shirt flashes in the peripheral of my vision. I shift to the left. I can either run towards the road, or back into the woods. If I run towards the road, I have a better chance of escaping April, but I'll more than likely be picked up by the police. If I run into the woods, I might be slower, but I also might be able to slip them both. I head towards the woods, forcing my aching thighs to move even faster up the slight slope. Sweat runs down my forehead, stinging my eyes and blurring my vision. I whip my head to the right as another red blur rushes through the trees, then to the left, sure that I saw something else. I swerve to the right to stop myself running straight into a tree, but in doing so, I lose precious seconds. April appears from between two trees. She's smiling as she sticks one foot out and catches my ankle.

I'm an easy target, unbalanced from the bindings on my wrists. I fall face down onto the hard earth, biting my tongue and hitting my forehead on a tree root. My mouth fills with blood and soil. I spit it out as I turn over. A small bundle of red and black pounces on me; straddling my waist with long legs, pinning my hands beneath her.

She lifts a large rock.

It's not the crash that appears in my mind, which surprises me. Whenever I'm stressed or upset, the crash always comes into my head. Not this time. It's a Sunday morning. I'm making breakfast for Stu as he's reading the paper. Emma has a bowl of porridge that she's smeared all over her face and her high chair. Stu is laughing at her and tickling her chin. It's what I lost, but it's also what I *had*. April never had this. She was never that little girl in the high chair. I'm luckier than most people in the world. I've had happiness.

I gaze up at April and I smile.

"I forgive you," I say.

APRIL

She goes over the plan one more time. Crush one of Mummy's sleeping pills and put it in the bottle of gin. Then take another and put it in the beer. Wait for Mum and Dad to drink the entire bottle and wait for them to pass out. Get the whiskey from the kitchen and pour it all over the sofa where they're asleep. Turn on all the gas rings on the cooker. Light the whiskey on fire. Run out of the house.

She thinks it should work. She heard Mum telling Dad about the plan one night. Mum was drunk, again, and yelling at her dad. "I'll drug you," she'd said. "I'll drug you and cover you in whiskey. I'll set you on fire and watch you burn. You're a good for nothing bastard and I want you dead."

April imagined her Mummy all scrunched over like a hunchback with spit flying from her mouth. She remembered how red faced and wrinkled she'd been. That night, April had written her mother's words into her journal. Then she'd sat and started to think carefully about what she'd heard. That's when she'd thought of the plan. She was cleverer than mum. She added the gas because it would look more like an accident, and in books and on TV, fires in homes were always about gas.

Plus, she knew about gas because her Mum would taunt her: "I'll leave the gas on while you're asleep. One spark and you'll go boom." Mum liked to tell her loved ones how she would murder them.

They look happy when they're asleep. Maybe I look happy when I sleep too, April thought. She didn't feel it though. She never felt happy. Maybe she doesn't even know what happiness is. People on television say they're happy. They smile and cry and hug people. She didn't do any of those things. But she's aware of her nerves, because her heart is going fast. It's a good plan, she reminds herself. She's thought of everything. She has to make sure that she's on the right side of the flames when the house starts burning. If she's not, she might get hurt and she doesn't want that. Only Mum and Dad should be hurt, because they keep hurting her and that has to stop. They have to be punished.

The whiskey smells horrible. It reminds her of when Dad hits her around the head and tells her to fuck off. She's not allowed to say those words but he can.

"Fuck. Fuck. Fuck," April says as she pours the whiskey over them.

She puts one of Mum's cigarettes in her mouth and lights it with a match. Then she cuts off a little of Mummy's hair, and Daddy's hair, and places it in her journal with the used match. She puts the little journal in her dressing gown pocket. They never found it, just like she knew they wouldn't. They don't pay attention to her, they don't care about anything she does or says, and they're too stupid to find her hiding place anyway.

Then she hurries into the kitchen and turns on the gas. She

leaves a trail of whiskey going into the kitchen, then throws the empty bottle on Mum's lap. April's heart goes pitter-patter as her mother rolls over in her sleep. But Mum doesn't wake, and April can't help but smile. That was the first time she'd felt scared. There was one night when she thought about calling it all off. She was in bed thinking about how the police might arrest her and put her in prison. But then she heard a noise downstairs and peeked through the bannisters on the landing. Mum was with another man. She decided then that it was worth the risk and she didn't care about getting caught. They deserve it.

She moves towards the door and lights a match. She throws it down onto the wet patch on the carpet where she poured the whiskey. It doesn't light. She tries it again and again. The matches keep going out when she throws them. She creeps forward, lights the match, and bends down. Her fingers shake as she places the match on the ground. The whiskey lights. But it catches the bottom of her dressing gown and she has to pat at it with her hands to stop it going up in flames. Her heart beats really hard as she flails her arms at the flames, whacking them down. She breathes a sigh of relief when they go out. Then she grins. Singeing the bottom of her dressing gown was a good move.

She waits until the fire gets going, watching with wide eyes as the sofa her parents sleep on catches fire. If the flames don't kill them, the smoke will. Then she grabs the telephone and calls 999, moving towards the door and away from the flames. She starts to cry, because she knows that's what they want to hear.

Mum leaps up and screams as she catches fire. April is frozen for a moment, watching the flames all over her skin, standing with her arms outstretched. She's like one of the *zombie monsters in the films they like to watch, April thinks. She watches as Mum takes two steps before falling to the floor, with her hands clawing at the carpet. Her wails are like nails on a chalkboard. April backs away from her, feeling for the door handle. There are sirens outside and it's time to go.*

She opens the door, and runs out into the cold air. It's a relief after the heat of the flames. She gently touches the bulge in her dressing gown that she knows is her journal. She needs to keep that close. She won't let anyone touch it.

The night is bright with the lights of the fire engine. As she's running, she sees a man in bright clothes step down from the engine. He crouches down and opens out his arms, waiting for her to run into them.

When he folds his arms around her, she knows that she has finished her plan. She's done it. She's got rid of them. Now she can find parents who don't deserve to die.

LAURA

Squinting at the phone on my dashboard, I take a bend too fast and almost lose control. My hands are shaking every time I change gear. I can't stop thinking about the journal. At first I'd thought it was a joke. I figured it was April messing with me by writing a fake journal. Then I found the match and the hair.

She was clever. So clever that it made me very afraid. Her diary was underneath the bed, but it was phoney. In it she'd written about how Matt and I hit her. None of it was true. She said that I locked her in the space under the stairs and beat her for stupid reasons like not cleaning up, or tidying her room, or because I was drunk. The diary confused me at first. I couldn't work out why she would say those things. That's when I decided to search her entire room.

It was only when I figured out the false back on her desk that I found the real journal, the one she's been writing in since she was seven years old. It's not a book I ever see her with around the house, this is something she has kept very secret. It's a small, dark blue book with a spine that has been

Sellotaped back together several times. I was afraid to turn the pages in case they fell apart.

She hasn't written in it often over the years. There's the terrifying plot to kill her parents, a plot that I realise is real. I remember when I was told her parents died in a fire. I felt for her. I loved her for what she had suffered. They were drunks who passed out with cigarettes and a bottle of whiskey spilled all over themselves, the gas from the stove left on in their drunken stupor. I knew what it was like to have drunks for parents. I knew what she'd suffered.

But I didn't know this.

In her journal there were charts documenting the amount of time I spent at work, alongside the amount of time I spent with April. She wrote sad and smiley faces next to them. Underneath those charts it said: NEEDS TO BE PUNISHED. The words made me shudder. Matt's whereabouts had been documented, too. April figured out the affairs long before I did. She'd jotted down every time Matt was physical with me. There were more accounts than I realised.

I'd repeated the past. I married my father.

But the journal wasn't the worst item I found in April's room. As clever as she was, she was still a thirteen-year-old child, and she wasn't half as good at hiding things as she thought.

I went through everything, and I found a shoe box hidden under a pile of clothes in her wardrobe. That's when I found the bodies of the mice she'd killed. Some of them were cut open, with their entrails pinned down with little corkboard pins. I dropped the box when I first opened it. I dropped it, and watched a stiff, dead-eyed mouse roll across the floor. Then I ran to the bathroom and I threw up.

My daughter.

How could I let this happen under my own roof? Why didn't I know? I'm a failure.

I brush away tears, and pull over behind the Ford. Now I know why the street seemed emptier, Hannah's car wasn't there. I'd read about April's plan in her journal. She'd decided to enlist Hannah with the sign and with a letter, then frame Hannah for Matt's murder. That's where she got lucky. Hannah ended up so involved with saving April from us, that she didn't see what was really going on. The police already think she's obsessed with us.

The passenger door of the Ford is flung open. I get out of the car, and examine my surroundings. We're next to the field that leads into the woods. Despite the warmth of midday, I shiver. This is where she has lured her victims.

I've already called the police, but now I need to do more. I need to be brave. This is my daughter, and my responsibility. If I'm the one who has failed her, I'm the one who truly needs to be punished. I'm going to confront her, and I'm going to stop her. I climb over the fence and into the field. That's when I see people running through the field. I have to get to them.

HANNAH

"I forgive you."

April pauses with the rock raised. She thinks I'm talking to her, but I'm talking to myself. All these years I've carried the blame. I was the one who was speeding. I was the one with the tears in my eyes so that I couldn't see. I was the one who missed a buckle on Emma's car seat. I know that Stu made it difficult, he was annoyed and pressuring me, but it was me who made the decision to drive recklessly. It was all me, and I've shouldered that for all these years.

Now I'm ready to let go. If I am going to die, I'm going to do it without this great blame pressing me down. I'm going to leave this world without the weight of that guilt.

But April has paused. Her eyes have changed. They are narrowing, as though she doesn't understand what is happening.

She raises the rock even higher. But now I have a slight opportunity. I have a sliver of time on my side. I twist myself to the left as the rock smashes down. It catches me, but it only scrapes some of the skin from my scalp. Using the momentum I gained from moving away from the rock, I rotate to the right, unbalancing April. She lets out a small cry as she falls onto the forest floor, allowing me to twist onto my belly and scramble away from her.

I push myself forwards with my legs and feet, my arms a hindrance underneath my weight. April is on her side, and the rock has fallen from her hands. There are sirens in the distance. I might live, but I won't escape arrest.

"Stop it, you're ruining everything!" April yells.

I twist onto my back and meet her eyes. I want to develop a connection with her, make her understand what she's trying to do. Maybe I can reason with her. "You want to kill me, but you have nothing to punish me for," I say. "If you kill me it's just murder, April. There's no reason to do it, only that you want to."

She clenches her fist and teeth, screws up her eyes like a child having a tantrum, and lets out a frustrated scream. "Why have you ruined it?" Then I see her gaze moving across the grass, searching for the stone.

I have to get away from her, because I want to live, and April isn't going to accept that. No, she's out for blood now. She's angry and nothing else will do. So I have to work hard at pushing myself along the ground, working my legs so that I keep moving. I'm still unbalanced with my hands tied beneath my body, and getting onto my feet will take up too many precious seconds. This is preservation now. I'm letting my instincts take over, moving in hurried, jerky movements.

April finds her stone, but the sirens are getting louder. She only has moments to murder me before the police arrive. If they see her kill me, she'll more than likely be taken into custody. I'm nauseated just thinking about April's age. She's too young for prison. She'll be put in some juvenile centre and released when she's an adult. I shudder.

I need to get on my feet. I need to run.

As April is coming for me, I get on my knees and lean forward so that my face is in the dirt. There, I can shift my weight back onto my heels and lean back on my feet, pushing up my body. I force my body up until I'm at full height, feeling the effort in my thighs. My head whips around, trying to find a flash of movement close by. What was that? My head whips around again. This time it's April running at me through the trees.

April's eyes are fixed on mine. She runs with her shoulders leaning forward, as though meaning to charge me down. Without my hands, I'm unbalanced, but I can still move out of her way. That's when I see the other flash of movement. I wasn't imagining things. We're not alone in the field. But April is determined. Her mouth is set into a grimace as she charges towards me. Her free hand is clenched, the other is wrapped around a rock. There's a slight trickle of blood coming from the corner of her mouth where she's bitten her lip. She's like a spectral waif, all pale and skinny, but with the face of a monster.

I don't move and I can see the flicker in April's eyes as she wonders why. She turns her head to the left, but it's too late. April doesn't make it. Before she can attack me, she's knocked to the ground. April's stone rolls out of her hand, and Laura pins April against the grass. As April squirms underneath her mother, Laura calmly takes each wrist in her hand. Laura has weight behind her, not just the weight of her body, but the years of caring for April. Years where she has dressed her, bathed her, cooked for her. Where she's told her off for not going to bed on time or for talking back. That spectral waif disappears before my eyes, leaving a teenage girl behind. I'm not sure which is the most frightening.

"That's enough," Laura says. "It stops now."

As the sirens finally make it onto the street, April starts to cry.

* * *

"When I found the mice, I came straight to find you," Laura says. She takes a sip of hospital tea and smiles weakly. "I'd put a GPS tracker on April's mobile phone. I forgot all about it until that moment. I'm sorry I didn't get there sooner."

"I'm sorry I didn't listen to you when you said that April lies," I reply. "How did the police interview go?"

"It was awful. I had to sit there and hear her tell lie after lie. The police know she's lying now. They've read her journal and seen the mice. They have the match from the house fire her parents died in. They have your witness testimony, and they found zip ties in her room. I can't believe it. She was my little girl. How could I not see it?" Laura shakes her head and I stay silent, letting her get out everything she needs to. "I keep thinking about the zip ties in her room. And the way she wrote everything in her journal. She was still just a kid, you know? For all her planning and plotting, and the way she hurt so many people, she still wasn't clever enough to destroy them, because at the end of the day, she was just a fucking kid."

"You can't blame yourself." But I know the words are useless. Laura will blame herself for as long as she feels the need to.

She sniffs and wipes her eyes. "I keep thinking that she learned it from me. I mean, I put on this act, too, you know? I pretend to be something I'm not. I'm from Rotherham, but I changed my accent to sound posher. I didn't want to sound like my parents because... because of what they were like. What if she learned all this from me?"

"It's not the same," I say.

"I had to change so I could make something of myself. But in the process I wonder if I made myself too detached, too cold. I pushed her away and she became a monster." Laura places a hand over her mouth. She clears her throat and seems to shake her feelings away. "But she's still my daughter. I'm going to stick by her. I'm going to visit her, and make sure she's treated right, because she's my daughter." She laughs. "I can't believe I'm saying that. A few days ago, I was regretting her even being in my life. Now, even after everything that has happened, I don't regret adopting her. I just regret not being able to stop her becoming..." She trails off and stares out into the distance.

"Maybe you never could," I reply. "Maybe it was in her DNA to begin with. You don't know anything for sure."

Laura gives me a weak smile and steps up from the visitor's chair. "Well, you get better now. How long are you in for?"

"I'm out this afternoon," I reply. "They wanted to keep an eye on me because of the concussion."

Laura winces slightly at the word. "Well, I'd better get back to Matt."

"Is there any change?"

"He's still in a coma. I'm hoping he wakes up so he can give his side of the story." Laura starts to leave, but before she goes, she adds. "I'm not going to stay with him. I realised what I'd done. I... my parents were drunks, and they hit me. I married a controlling man with a temper. I repeated the cycle."

"I married a man with a wandering eye," I reply. "My father cheated on my mother, and my husband did the same to me. It's hard not to repeat history. But someone has to break the cycle. It'd may as well be us."

Laura is still nodding her head as she leaves the hospital room. Somehow I already know that we'll never see each other again. But I wish her well.

That afternoon, after I'm discharged from the hospital, I drive myself to a place I haven't visited in a long time. The weather is perfect for it. On the way, I call at a garage and pick the brightest bunch of flowers I can find. As I drive, I lean back against my driver's seat, and let one hand rest on my knee like I used to do on a summery day. The windows are down, my car smells like flowers, and the sun warms my skin.

I drive slowly through the cemetery, remembering each turn as though the directions are carved into my being. The gravestone is wide, marble, and a warm grey. Their names are etched in gold. James chose the spot, but he did it well. They're high up, so that the valley stretches out below them. Stu always loved to be in high, windy places where he could oversee the surrounding countryside. He was from a small village in the Peak District, and he never really got out of that small village mentality. He loved beauty. He loved the peaks and valleys of our country. He would have loved this spot.

Next to them is a dark mahogany bench. I remember it well from the funeral. I sit there for a while, arranging the flowers, cutting off leaves, trimming stalks, placing them into the pot that fits onto the grave stone. James has been here. He's cleaned up, and removed old flowers. I knew he would. I know he misses Emma almost as much as I do. He misses me, too, because I've not been me for a long time.

I could stay here all day and watch the sun go down, but Stu wouldn't want me to linger. I've lingered long enough, living in the half-life of grief. It's time to leave this place.

I take a few more moments to think. I take a deep breath, bringing with it the smell of the lilies in my bouquet, and the freshly mown grass from a plot further up the cemetery. There's no tightness in my chest anymore. Sometimes, when I close my eyes, I see April poised with the rock in her hands, her eyes narrowing as she tries to understand why I would forgive her. I should hate April for what she put me through, and I should be more anxious than ever. But I don't feel either of those things. She awakened me. I've finally woken up from the nightmare that kept me confined to my house. I might not have saved April, but I saved myself.

When the flowers are arranged, I put the wrapper and the trimmings into the bin, and make my way back to my car. They aren't there, Stu and Emma, I don't feel their presence in their graves. Just like I'm not really in number 73 Cavendish Street, I'm finally somewhere else.

EPILOGUE
APRIL

This is all stupid. They're stupid. They think they can figure me out with their questions. They lock me up in my room so I don't hurt others. They make me eat with plastic cutlery so I don't hurt myself. I'm not allowed to talk to other people because I'm a bad influence. They treat me like I'm a crazy monster who's going to attack them at any moment. And every day, they ask me the same questions.

"Why do you feel the need to punish people, April?" she asks. It's Dr. Humphries this time. I don't like her. She has these tiny, icy blue eyes that stare right through you. Sometimes she calls herself Humphries, and I think that is way creepier than anything I've done.

I shrug. "Someone has to."

"Do you like to outwit people? Do you like to prove your intelligence?"

I could outwit you, I think. I'm smarter than everyone in here. Who else thought of the plan to kill their parents and not get caught? If it hadn't been for Laura and Hannah... I never thought of that. I never thought of Hannah fighting back. She was so weak, so easily controlled. Laura surprised me with the GPS thing. Well played, Laura.

"No," I lie. "I don't need to *prove* anything."

Dr. Humphries gets this little smile on her face that I totally want to wipe away with my fist. But I tell myself there's no point. I don't like to be violent for no reason. I like my violence to have a *good* reason, like teaching Hannah a lesson.

"Why did you kill your parents?"

I roll my eyes. "You know why. They were scum. They deserved it. In fact, they had it coming. I saved them, anyway."

"What do you mean?"

"They drank every day and it was disgusting. They were slowly poisoning their bodies. I may have only been eight, but I still understood that they were going to drink themselves to death. I saved them years of agony."

"So you believe that you did them a favour. You don't think you did anything wrong?"

"I know I broke the *law*. You people keep telling me that. But they deserved it. I don't know how many more times I can tell you that."

"We keep going over this because you see the world differently to other people, April. You need to understand that the things you say and do aren't normal. Most girls your age have a better understanding of empathy and morality." Humphries leans back in her chair. She always sits a few feet away from me, and she always glances nervously towards the door as though planning her exit. If I said "boo", she'd crap her pants. "What about your neighbour, Hannah Abbott?"

"What about her?"

"She tried to help you. Everything she did was to try and save you from an abusive home. But you manipulated, kidnapped, and assaulted her. None of that was punishment."

"I didn't intend to involve her. I was going to use Laura."

"What changed?"

"Laura was never around. When she was, I never knew how to make her do what I wanted." Laura never did what was expected. I would stay quiet, thinking she'd feel sorry for me, but she'd get suspicious instead. Then I'd leave my fake diary out for her to read, but she wouldn't touch it. I knew early on that I'd never get Laura to do what I wanted. That's when I started writing Laura into my fake diary. When the police came, I wanted her arrested too.

"So you used Hannah to try and kill your father, who you thought deserved to die?"

"He's a steroid taking, cheating, wife-beater, so yeah." I refuse to feel bad about what I did to Matt. He deserved that conk on the head, and he deserves the brain damage he got from it. It was a shame he woke up, though. I could have done without his statement to the police.

"Why are you smiling?" she asks.

I shrug. I'm thinking about the stupid expression on Matt's face as he fell to the floor of the shed. Then I think about the sound his skull made when I hit him for the second time.

"April there's one other thing we've not discussed yet.

You've been here for over a month now and we've discussed your actions towards people at length. We've come to understand that you have a very rigid sense of right and wrong, and that you believe people should be punished in very extreme ways. What we haven't discussed is your treatment of animals. Where did you get the mice from?"

"The woods a few streets away. Sometimes I'd sneak out of the house while Matt was cheating on Laura. I'd climb over the back fence and cut through a footpath near the field. I got quite good at catching them. I found the old shed and inside there were some traps, so I used them to catch the mice."

"Why didn't you keep them in the shed? Why did you take them home?" she asks.

"I..." I hadn't thought about that. It seemed like the right thing to do at the time. I did kill some of them in the shed, but I knew I only had a few hours before Matt came home, so I used to take them home and put them in a shoe box. Sometimes I let them starve, and would open the box at night to see what they looked like after a few days. Sometimes I played with them. Sometimes I killed them right away.

"April, did part of you want to get caught?"

"No," I say. "I wanted my plan to succeed."

"Are you sure? Because you didn't make it very hard for Laura to find everything when she searched your room."

"I didn't think she'd bother. She didn't give a shit about me, so why would she bother searching my room?"

"April, why did you kill the mice?"

"Because I like to watch squirming things go still."

THE END

* * *

SAVING APRIL was originally published on the 29th March 2016 by Kindle Press. Due to a rights reversion it was self-published in 2020.

ALSO BY SARAH A. DENZIL

Three For A Girl (Isabel Fielding book three)

The Isabel Fielding Boxed Set

-

Supernatural Suspense

You Are Invited

-

Short suspenseful reads

They Are Liars: A novella

Aiden's Story (a SILENT CHILD short story)

Harborside Hatred (A Liars Island novella)

A Quiet Wife

About the Author

Sarah A. Denzil is a British suspense writer from Derbyshire. Her books include SILENT CHILD, which has topped the kindle charts in the UK, US, and Australia. SAVING APRIL and THE BROKEN ONES are both top thirty bestsellers in the US and UK Amazon charts.

Combined, her self-published and published books, along with audiobooks and foreign translations, have sold over one million copies worldwide.

Sarah lives in Yorkshire with her husband, enjoying the scenic countryside and rather unpredictable weather. She loves to write moody, psychological books with plenty of twists and turns.

To stay updated, join the mailing list for new release announcements and special offers.

Writing as Sarah Dalton - http://www.sarahdaltonbooks.com/

Printed in Great Britain
by Amazon